Chihuahua Enchilada

Colleen Rae

CHIHUAHUA ENCHILADA
© Colleen Rae, 2011

Cover art by Colleen Rae
Book design by Jo-Anne Rosen

ISBN: 978-1-931002-96-7

Library of Congress Control Number: 2011927038

Wordrunner Press
Petaluma, California

Acknowledgements

Without the people who were readers for this novel and my professional editor, Roberto de Haro, I could never have pulled off this sequel, *Chihuahua Enchilada*. My thanks to Roberto, my friend and editor, for his many constructive and important suggestions and his superb line and copy editing. Readers Kathryn Jennings, an ESL teacher, Christie Nelson, author of *Woodstock*, and Paula Conrad, a consummate reader, all friends who were not afraid to critique my work to the ninth degree, added extra insights to the book. Lawrence Hippler, author of *The New Road*, a new online acquaintance whom I've never met, graciously consented to be a reader also, and made many important suggestions. My skill with the beautiful language of Spanish was sadly lacking. Both Roberto de Haro and Kathryn Jennings gave me advice on the Spanish language. Roberto de Haro made several corrections to the finished Spanish written in this novel.

Thanks to Joe Miller of Needles, California, an ex-policeman, whom I overlooked thanking for his expert advice on firearms in my first novel, *Mohave Mambo*. Thanks Joe and please forgive me.

A big thanks to Annette Cress and Reva Basch for a superb job of proof-reading the manuscript, and a grateful thank you to Jo-Anne Rosen for her excellent job of formatting this novel in preparation for printing. Also thanks to friend Jerry Hill for his research information and advice on firearms and handguns. Roberto de Haro also gave me advice on handguns.

I hope everyone who turns these pages enjoy this book as much as I've enjoyed writing it.

This book is dedicated to

my children, Lauren and Marc.

Contents

CHIHUAHUA ENCHILADA

A novel

by

Colleen Rae

Prologue

*J*ack caught her from behind and clamped his hand over her mouth. She was strong and struggled, making snarling noises, trying to bite his hand. Reaching up, sharp nails tore a long gash in his cheek.

"God damn it," he swore.

He stuck the point of the knife into the side of her neck just below the ear, cutting the carotid artery. Her trachea cracked like scaffolding falling in the wind as he pulled the knife across it. Blood spurted from her artery, gushing on his plastic hospital coat. He had been told to make it look like a random killing.

He dropped her to the sidewalk and dragged her over to the dumpster sitting beside the street. Long dark hair blew in the night breeze when he picked her up. Already her blue blouse and jeans were soaked red. He tossed her into the receptacle like so much garbage. Taking off the coat, he threw that in after the body.

Jack Marchetti had only arrived in Chihuahua, México that afternoon. He had taken a seedy hotel room downtown for a few days, visited his contact, Juan, and tracked down his 'hit.' Now he could go back to the room and catch a few hours sleep. A quick stop at the Chihuahua Enchilada Restaurante across from his hotel and he'd be back on the road driving north to the border. This had been a fast trip; he wished they all went this well. Guido would be pleased with the speed with which he'd executed this job.

PART I
Unexplored Terrain

1981

$\mathcal{H}$e was the first man Lola had ever loved. Oh, she'd had sex before; the traumatic abuse she experienced at the hands of her father when she was a child and a few fumbling encounters with young men she had dated. But Lenny Elmwood was the first man with whom she'd really enjoyed sex.

She had tried many times to put Lenny out of her mind but here she was traveling on this lonely road with her friend from Arizona, Sherry Brown, on the outskirts of Chihuahua, México, to visit Lenny. She hadn't seen him in ten years, and he had no idea she was coming.

She remembered their mad, passionate love-making, their serious late-night talks about playwrights and philosophers like Sartre and Nietzsche. Both Lenny and Lola had been activists against the Vietnam War. She had been crazy about him, and at the same time, gripped by a fear to commit to a long-term relationship.

He had been so down to earth; he would come bursting through her door, see her in her bra and panties and quip, "No need to put clothes on for me, I'm just going to take them off." He was open and loving. She, on the other hand, was enigmatic and mercurial. One minute she wanted him, the next she wasn't sure.

Her attention was back on the road she was driving as she meandered through fields of sienna-hued
earth and high desert landscapes as far as her vision
would allow. The aridness of the land reminded Lola
of Arizona, the place she and Sherry had just left. She
continued following the directions that Lenny had sent
her years ago.

What if he'd moved and didn't live here anymore?
Or perhaps he wouldn't be delighted at her unexpected
visit. After all, she had broken up with him. Then one
day he was gone. He'd sent his new address in México
for her in care of general delivery at the post office in
West Los Angeles. She might never have received it
if she hadn't gone to pick up a package and the postal
clerk recognized her name and handed her the letter
from Lenny. She said it had been there for a couple of
weeks.

Beside her in the passenger seat, Sherry was silent,
Lenny's written directions in hand, a little ragged after
all these years, somehow sensing Lola's sudden unease
at meeting her old love.

She must have been crazy to think he would welcome her after all this time. She and Sherry needed a
place to go for a while to keep a low profile, and she
thought México would be far enough away from any
Vegas connection.

The VW bumped and danced along the main highway entering Chihuahua from the north. Chihuahua
sits on a high plain, 1400 feet above sea level, nearly
surrounded by the Sierra Madre range. Scrub brush,

Cholla cactus, *Ocotillo*, with their brilliant red-orange blossoms, and *Saguaro* cactus were scattered across the mesa before her. Through the open window, her dark hair flying in the wind like a cactus wren, Lola could smell the sweet scent of desert lavender. The Blue *Chia* splashed across the floor of the plain, gracing the landscape with its indigo hues and pungent aroma. Golden Mexican poppies and desert marigolds appeared along the roadside, absorbing the radiant heat of the sun, painting the vista like a Van Gogh landscape.

Suddenly Sherry came to life. "Turn off the main roadway onto a smaller road right here."

After two miles, the girls saw a small sign reading Vista de Pajaro (a bird's eye view). They turned down a dirt road. An adobe house came into view featuring a veranda across the width of the structure. A large barn and a chicken coop could be seen in the back yard. Several free-range chickens roamed the grounds. Lola spied a beautifully landscaped cactus garden in the front yard, spring blossoms spilling across the sandy soil. The garden had Lenny's magic touch. A Ford pick-up stood beside the garage. They had arrived.

Lola took a deep breath and bit her cuticle.

Sherry reached over and patted her arm. "It will be all right, girl. If he doesn't seem happy to see you, we'll find a motel and stay the night. Don't worry. Tomorrow we'll decide where to go from here."

Lola smiled at Sherry as she got out of the little car and stretched her long legs. She was resigned to whatever the outcome. If he didn't want to see her, she wouldn't blame him. They walked up the stone walk and knocked on the wooden door. The door opened.

His face was like she'd seen it a thousand times in her dreams; firm jaw line, those wonderful sea-green eyes, and the full lips.

"Lola! My God!" He blurted, "I thought you were dead!"

⧓

*T*hey all stood staring at one another in a state of shock.

When Lenny recovered somewhat, he placed his hand firmly on her arm and pulled her inside. He looked at Sherry curiously. She stood a good four inches shorter than Lola.

"This is my…friend…Sherry," Lola stammered.

Lenny nodded in acknowledgement. "Damn! What are you doing here?" He backed into the entry way and preceded them down two steps to the sunken living room.

Lola felt her knees about to give way. A wave of dizziness enveloped her as she grabbed the nearest chair back. She reached the couch and sat down hard, still reeling from Lenny's greeting… "I thought you were dead!"

For some reason the memory of how they had met ten years ago flashed across her brain like an old movie. She could see herself going into the Laundromat with her basket of clothes and walking near this man with deep green eyes, a full head of blond wavy hair, and a beautiful German shepherd lying relaxed on the floor beside him. He and the dog had attracted her. She remembered putting down her basket, leaning down, and after first letting the animal smell the back of her hand, petting the lovely dog on the head. She never touched strange dogs. That was one of the ways in which she stayed alert, keeping herself safe from dangers in the world.

He looked up at her and smiled, full lips parted, and said, "Sheba never likes strangers. I'm surprised she let you touch her."

"I never touch strange dogs. It must have been some invisible pull between us." Lola said, smiling also.

Sheba stood up and nudged her head beneath Lola's palm. She and the young man laughed.

"She certainly is behaving like she likes you. My name is Lenny. What's yours?"

She stared into his green eyes. "Lola." For a few seconds they looked at each other. Lola picked up her basket and began putting her clothes in the washer.

Lenny walked over to her. "How about getting a cup of coffee while we wait for our clothes?"

Lola found herself being led across the street to an open air café where Sheba could lie beside their table. They had talked intensely for two hours, with no sense of time, and nearly forgot about their clothes. A date was made for the next night and for the next year she and Lenny were inseparable.

He made his living as a landscape designer. Since she had run away from home at seventeen, Lola had been giving dance lessons at an Arthur Murray Studio in the evenings, and was a cashier at a drugstore by day. It made her a living; she had not yet decided what to do with her life.

She and Lenny never moved in together. When it became clear that they were spending every night at either his place or hers, they discussed living together, but suddenly Lola got cold feet and packed up her belongings one morning after he'd left, and moved to another studio apartment.

She had kept the same phone number though, and when he called her a few days later, she explained that she was having doubts about their being together as a couple and needed some time apart.

Lenny said he was very hurt and hung up on her. They only saw each other a few more times after that, at the Laundromat. Then he was gone.

His voice broke into her memories. "What are you doing here?" he repeated. The fierceness in his eyes seemed to confirm her mistake in coming.

"I'm sorry, Lenny. I thought we were old friends and I…thought…Sherry and I needed to get out of the states for awhile."

"Are you in trouble?" he asked, his eyes never leaving her face.

"Not anymore. I'll tell you all about it later." Suddenly she thought of his greeting. "What do you mean you thought I was dead?"

Lenny wiped his forehead with the back of his hand. "I ran into an old friend from L.A. who had been living in Vegas. He said he'd heard my ex-girlfriend had been killed by…certain factions in Las Vegas."

Lola was stunned. Had the Mob put out this information? And if so, why?

Sherry had taken a seat protectively close to Lola on the couch, their shoulders touching. Lenny disappeared into the kitchen and returned carrying a tray with three sweating bottles of *cerveza*. Slices of lime were stuck over the rims of the bottles. He set the tray on the table and made another trip to the kitchen, returning with chips and a bowl of salsa.

Lola wasn't hungry but Sherry dug into the chips. "Thanks," Lola said.

Sherry echoed Lola's thanks between bites.

Lola picked up her Dos Equis, poked the lime slice down the neck of the bottle and took a long swig.

"Did your friend tell you where he got that information?" Lenny didn't know about her frightening adventure in Mohave Valley and how the hit man had tracked her down and nearly blown her brains out before her friend Pat had shot him dead.

Lenny shook his head. "No, he didn't."

Sherry glanced at Lola, shoving her long blonde hair behind one shoulder. "The Mob has been looking for Lola for a long time. They sent a hit man to Arizona to kill her. When he failed, and was killed, Lola was afraid they might send someone else to finish the job."

"So maybe the Mob put out the false info to flush her out," Lenny suggested.

Sherry shrugged. "Could be."

"I thought if Sherry and I could visit you for a few

days—we won't stay too long—we could sidetrack whoever might be following me. We have money; we won't be a burden to you." Lola took a deep breath.

"Well…I guess you can stay for a while." Lenny took a swig from his *cerveza*.

She gave him a smile.

Lenny did not smile back. "There is one thing I need to tell you. I…have a girlfriend, Gloria. She stays over with me a couple of nights a week."

Lola felt her pulse quicken. "Of course, Lenny. I didn't mean that…Well, you don't have to tell her our history. We are just a couple of friends of yours from the States visiting. Won't that do?"

He nodded. "Yep."

A long silence made Lola uncomfortable. "Maybe we should just be on our way." She looked at Sherry.

Sherry nodded.

Lenny got up. "No, you're here now. Stay for a while. You must be tired from the driving."

Lola looked carefully at Lenny. "Sure?"

He nodded.

"Can we get a shower and change our clothes? We're both kind of travel-weary," she said.

"Sure. Come on down the hall and I'll show you the other room."

"I'll get the suitcases, Lola," Sherry called as she went out the door.

"Don't forget the saddle bags," Lola called back.

Lola followed Lenny down the hall while Sherry made a trip to the VW for the luggage. Lenny showed her into a large sunny room, the twin beds at one end with a dresser between them, and a couch, table and chair at the other end. At the open window a jasmine vine with luscious-smelling white blossoms spilled inside. On the wall were posters of long-ago bullfighters from México's past.

Lola took a deep breath, inhaling the jasmine aroma. "It's lovely, Lenny. Thanks."

"The beds need sheets. Haven't had any guests lately." He was standing so close to her she could feel his warm breath on her arm. He looked at her dark eyes and honey skin. Suddenly he pulled her into his arms. "Just a hug for an old friend. I'm so glad you're alive."

When the headiness from his hug had passed, she said, "Me, too."

Sherry appeared at the doorway carrying two suitcases. "I have to go back for the saddle bags."

"Here, I'll get the rest," Lenny offered, and was out the door before either Sherry or Lola could say a word.

Sherry's eyebrows went up. "Will he look inside?"

Lola shook her head. "No, I don't think so. But if he does, we'll tell him we robbed a bank."

That tickled them and when Lenny returned they were giggling in fits of laughter.

"What did I miss," he asked, smiling for the first time, their laughter infecting him.

"Not much. We're kind of slap-happy from travel. We'll be better company when we shower," Lola said.

"Say, what's so heavy in these saddle bags?" Lenny asked, as he tossed them on the bed.

Sherry looked at Lola. "Money — we robbed a bank." Lola said, with a sober expression.

Lenny looked from one to the other for a long moment. "No shit?"

Sherry was the first to break out laughing. "No, no, tell him Lola."

Through her laughter Lola explained. "We befriended an old desert rat in Arizona, name of Marshmallow. He was a sweet old guy; we both loved him," Lola's voice wavered. "Before he died he bequeathed his small fortune to us as well as his ancient Airstream trailer, equally ancient Ford truck and the parcel of land where he lived. Sherry and I cashed our checks before leaving Mohave Valley and put the cash in the saddle bags."

Lenny's mouth was open in surprise by the time Lola had finished the story.

"We left instructions to sell the trailer, land and truck," Sherry added.

"Well, I'll be damned," he said thoughtfully. After a moment, he said, "may I ask how much you have stashed in those bags?"

"Approximately $20,000."

The whistle Lenny made was clear and loud. "I have a safe in the house. It really isn't smart to have that much money where someone could find it. I would like to say Gloria is above snooping in your stuff, but I can't."

"Good idea. Okay, Sherry?"

Sherry nodded. "If you trust Lenny, so do I."

Lenny picked up the two saddle bags from the bed. "Follow me." He led the girls to his master bedroom and through the walk-in closet to the side wall. Pulling a row of clothes aside, he reached upward and pushed a button and the panel slide back, exposing a black metal safe the size of a small freezer. He twirled the dial a couple of times and the door popped open. Pulling out a deep drawer he handed it to Lola. "Put your money in here."

Lola started taking out the stacks of money held together with rubber bands. When she had emptied her bag, she started on Sherry's, leaving the rubber bands on her money.

Lenny stood silently watching in wonder, shaking his head.

When Lola finished, Lenny put the drawer back in the safe and swung the door shut. With a flourish he twirled the dial. He pulled the panel closed and rear-ranged the clothes. No one would ever suspect what the wall held.

Before the three of them walked out of Lenny's bedroom, Lola cast a quick look around. A double wide bed, unmade, stood against one wall. Two end tables with identical lamps on either side, a large dresser on the other wall with a small TV on top. That was all she had time to see.

"The shower's down the hall. Don't use too much hot water, or the second person will have a cold one."

"You go first, Sherry," Lola said. "Save me some warm water."

At the girl's room, Lola stopped and turned to Lenny. "Thanks."

"Sure. The combo is my birthday. Do you remember?" He asked, his face serious.

Lola was surprised. He was giving her the combination. She reached back into her memory. March 12, 1957. "The combo is 3-12-57?"

He placed his hand on her shoulder. "You have a good memory." Lenny smiled for the second time.

"I promise you we won't be any trouble. We won't upset your girlfriend, Gloria. We'll be gone in a few days."

Lenny nodded. "I don't like remembering all the old shit I went through when we broke up."

"I understand. We won't talk about that. That's the past."

Lenny walked to the kitchen. Lola went into the guest room and threw herself on one of the twin beds. Perhaps coming here wasn't such a great idea, after all. Did she want to stir up all those old feelings? And Lenny seemed less than delighted at their visit.

⧓

After the girls had bathed and changed clothes (Lola had taken special care with what she wore, slipping on a blue peasant blouse and fresh jeans that hugged her figure), they joined Lenny in the living room.

"Why don't we go into town and get a bite to eat? I have a special place I go. They make great enchiladas."

Lola looked at Sherry and they both nodded vigorously. By now Lola's appetite had returned and she was hungry.

The three of them piled into Lenny's truck, Sherry crammed into the middle with the gearshift between her knees.

The *restaurante* was a good-sized *cantina* in the downtown district by the name of Chihuahua Enchilada. The aroma wafting from the kitchen would make an anorexic hungry. The tables sported plastic tablecloths, metal silverware and paper plates, but the enchiladas, according to Lenny, and the vegetarian tostadas, which was what Lola ordered, were first class.

After they had sated their appetites and were finishing their Dos Equis', Lola said, "Tell me about your girlfriend."

Lenny looked away and said, "Not much to tell. Gloria is a dancer in a stage show downtown. She was raised here, her parents were in the drug smuggling business and are both incarcerated. She had a tough upbringing."

"You sure like your dancers, don't you?" Lola said with a smile.

Lenny grinned back and nodded. "She never made the big money that you must have made in Vegas." Lola had told him about her life in Vegas.

"I made good money there but I didn't save much." Returning to the subject of Gloria, Lola asked, "When do we get to meet her?"

"I'm sure as soon as she hears I have two beautiful female house guests she'll be right over," Lenny replied.

"Is she the jealous type?" Sherry asked.

Lenny waved his hand in the air. "Yeah, you could say that. When she gets mad she starts yelling in rapid

Spanish. I don't understand half of what she says, fortunately for me."

"You can assure her she has nothing to worry about with either Sherry or me," Lola said straight-faced. "I'm concerned about why your friend in Vegas heard I was dead."

"Yeah, me too," Sherry chimed in.

"I don't know, but I think you're far enough away from there to be safe. We won't advertise your name around town. No one needs to know you're here."

"Thanks, Lenny." Lola smiled at him and looked into those green eyes.

He gave her a cool smile back.

The knowledge that Lenny had a woman in his life left her strangely uncomfortable. What did she expect? That he would welcome her with amorous arms? That he was still interested after ten years? She tried to remind herself of her previous admonition in Mohave Valley when she first met Billy Jim, the man she'd lived with for a little over a year. She wasn't ready for another man in her life. That proved to be true then. This time she would heed her own warning.

⧓

*L*enny lay back on his bed against the pillows and thought of Lola. What a shock, her showing up like that! She had taken him so unawares when she appeared at the door. His feelings were all jumbled up. He didn't know if he was glad to see her again, or unhappy at her sudden visit. He saw pain in her lovely dark eyes, troubled at the news he had shared, that he'd heard she was dead. When his friend told him she'd been killed in Las Vegas, he realized he had made a terrible mistake in giving in to his hurt pride and taking off instead of trying to get her back. His life had taken quite a few twists in the last ten years since they'd parted. He thought he'd put her behind him. But here she was again, in his life.

The clock on his table showed it was 11 a.m. Climbing out of bed, he threw on some clothes and went to the kitchen to make coffee. He put on the coffee, and took down three cups from the cupboard. All was quiet; the girls were still sleeping. They'd had quite a night last evening, celebrating late, smoking a little primo Michoacán weed he'd reserved for special occasions.

Lola had told him about her life since she'd left him; Sherry had told about hers. He'd heard all about Lola's year-long stay in Mohave Valley; witnessing the murder of her boyfriend in Las Vegas, leaving her job as an exotic dancer and Las Vegas and hiding out in a small Arizona town. Her eventual meeting and love affair with Billy Jim, and the culmination of the killer's search for her and his death at the hands of her friend and bar owner, Pat Sweeney. When they could smoke no more, and ran out of words, they hit the sack around 3 a.m.

The coffee started to perc and Lola appeared in the doorway in a pink tee-shirt and jeans, her hair uncombed. She looked very becoming with it all messed up.

"Morning," Lenny said.

Lola nodded, and yawned. "Sorry I'm not much company until I have my first cup of coffee."

"I remember," Lenny replied.

She turned toward him and smiled the way she used to smile, brushing the bangs off her forehead.

Lenny poured two cups of coffee. He handed one to Lola.

Lola took a chair at the table and Lenny sat across from her.

To change the subject, Lenny asked, "Want a tour of the town? There's not much to see. A nice university, a couple of museums; this is mostly an industrial town. I chose it because not too many tourists come here. I figured I could get lost in the crowd."

Lola looked at him closely. "Why did you need to get lost in the crowd?"

"No particular reason. Except I wanted to start over."

"And have you?"

Lenny nodded. A silence between them began and stretched on until Sherry came into the kitchen.

"Hope I'm not interrupting anything." She noticed their silence as she went to the counter and poured herself a cup of coffee.

"You're not. How about some bacon and eggs?" Lenny asked, heading for the refrigerator.

"Sounds good. I'll pass on the bacon." Lola said.

Lenny turned to face her. "Still a vegetarian?"

She nodded.

"But I'm not, and I'm hungry," Sherry chimed in. "I'll cook if you want."

"Fine. Haven't had a woman cook for me in quite a while."

"Doesn't Gloria cook?" Lola asked.

"Nope. We usually go out to eat."

"By the way," Lola said, "When can we expect to meet her? Will she be dropping by?"

"I never know. She may call or just come by."

Sherry cooked up some scrambled eggs and bacon and toast, and the three of them sat down to breakfast.

Lenny was wondering how Gloria would take the news that he had two women, one from his past, visiting him. He wasn't really worried; if she didn't like it she could stay away until Lola and Sherry left.

≳≲

*T*he next day Lenny called his archaeology instructor, *Profesor* Gilberto, to make an appointment at 11:30 a.m. for lunch. They drove to the campus in downtown Chihuahua, parked and walked to Doctor Barry Gilberto's office.

The sun was high in the sky; the colors of the campus landscaping were greener, with several more subtle hues this morning than Lenny was used to seeing. Or so it seemed to him. The dahlias around the *profesor's* office sparkled like pink cotton candy and smelled luscious.

When they entered the *profesor's* office, the girls saw a tall man with a dark beard laced with white and a full head of matching hair.

"*Profesor* Gilberto, this is an old friend, Lola Raines Morales, and her friend, Sherry Brown."

Each of the girls shook his hand. "Pleased to meet you, *Profesor*," Lola acknowledged.

"Please be seated, ladies." The *profesor* spoke perfect English. "Welcome to Chihuahua. Are you on vacation? And where are you from?" The man was vibrant in his manner and spoke quickly in a melodic low voice.

"We are here to visit Lenny," Lola said. "He and I are old friends from our Los Angeles days."

"It's very nice to meet any of Lenny's friends. Since he only took a few classes with me, I haven't seen him as often as I would like." He looked closely at Sherry. "Where are you from, Sherry?"

"I grew up in Arizona, never been anywhere else. When Lola decided to come to México, I thought it would be good to see some other parts of the world."

"So right, my dear," the *profesor* said. "México is very beautiful and diverse in many ways." Changing the subject, the *profesor* said, "Regarding lunch, we could eat in the university cafeteria. They serve very good food. Is that okay?"

"Of course, sir," Lenny said.

The four of them walked downstairs to the cafeteria and stood in line with several teachers and students. They found an empty table and sat down to eat. Lola ordered a plate of corn enchiladas, Sherry had tamales and beans, and Lenny and *Profesor* Gilberto picked out plates of rice, beans, tamales and tacos. All chose Royal Crown colas to wash down the food.

"Has Lenny taken you to see any of the museums in town?" *Profesor* Gilberto asked.

"Not yet," Lola answered.

"That was what we were going to do this afternoon," Lenny replied.

"I would recommend going to the Museo de Historia del Estado de Chihuahua. That's a pretty impressive display of historical documents. Then we have an art museum here. And there is also an archaeology museum right here on campus. That should fill an afternoon," the *profesor* laughed. "Wish I could go with you, but I have papers to correct."

"Maybe another time we can have dinner together?" Lenny asked.

"Of course, I would love that. Since my wife passed away, I get tired of eating alone. Let's plan that very soon."

"I'm sorry, *Profesor*, about your wife," Lola commented.

The *profesor* stopped eating. "Thank you. She's been gone four years now, and I still miss her. When a man finds a woman he loves dearly, he should keep her with him as long as possible. She was ill the last year of her life, but I took a sabbatical and cared for her myself."

Lenny's eyes wandered to Lola's across the table, and then darted away. Lola avoided his eyes. Sherry saw Lenny's look and gently jabbed Lola in the elbow. Lola nudged her back.

"How long do you girls plan on staying in Chihuahua?" the *profesor* asked.

Lola shrugged. "We aren't sure, maybe a few days."

"Have the girls met your friend, Gloria?" the *profesor* inquired.

Lenny shook his head. "Not yet. She hasn't called or come over in the last week. It isn't like her."

"Maybe she's heard about your two beautiful visitors from the States," the *profesor* said with a twinkle in his eye.

"I doubt it; I think she would have been right over, if she had heard about that. I've tried calling her and she's never home."

"We don't want to put a crimp in Lenny's love life," Lola said with a smile.

"From what Lenny told me about her, she's a free spirit. She comes and goes as she pleases."

Lenny nodded. "Yeah, that's okay, but I guess it doesn't occur to her that I might worry."

"I'm sure she'll turn up on your doorstep soon." The *profesor* slapped Lenny gently on the back. "I need to get back to the office. Give me a call soon and we will plan a dinner out together. It was so nice meeting you two lovely girls. *Hasta luego.*" *Profesor* Gilberto stood and took his plate to the dirty dishes rack, then waved as he left the cafeteria.

Lenny, Sherry, and Lola racked their dishes, and headed back to Lola's VW.

The rest of the afternoon was spent viewing artifacts in the university museum, and then touring the Historia de Chihuahua Museo. They returned to the ranch around four o'clock. Not wanting to go out again, Lenny brought out chips, salsa and cervezas, and that was their dinner.

≋

*L*ola and Sherry had been at Lenny's for a week. During that time Lenny's girlfriend Gloria had not dropped in or called. He had warmed up to Lola somewhat and was the perfect host to Sherry, taking them around and showing them the city.

Lenny called a friend of his, Clint Gonzales, and invited him over to meet the girls.

Clint pulled into Lenny's yard in a red Corvette. Since Lenny had said Clint was his weed connection, Lola thought driving a red car might not be the wisest choice, but she kept that opinion to herself.

He walked in the front door that stood wide open. Clint was five eleven, tall for a part *Mestizo*—half Spanish and Indian—and moved with the grace of a jungle cat. Long straight hair tied back in a pony tail, thick dark brows that nestled over dark flashing eyes. A big smile showed even white teeth. Clint was a good-looking guy who attracted women. He took off his cowboy hat and tossed it on the chair.

"Clint, this is Lola and Sherry. Lola is an old friend and Sherry is a new one," Lenny said.

"*Hola, chicas,*" Clint said. "Welcome to Chihuahua." His eyes lingered appreciatively on Sherry, noticing her curvaceous figure and long blonde hair.

Lola and Sherry smiled, greeted Clint and took seats on the couch. Lenny pulled up a chair next to the coffee table. Clint took the ottoman beside the table and pulled out a joint. "I brought some of my primo Acapulco Gold. It just came in the other day. It's really dynamite." He lit the joint, and passed it to Lola.

She took a hit and passed it to Sherry. By the time the joint reached Lenny both the girls were coughing.

"Wow, that is something else," Sherry said.

"What are you girls doin' down here?" Clint asked.

"Uh…We decided to come south and visit Lenny," Lola said.

"Where you from?"

"We're from Arizona most recently. Near the Colorado River," Sherry answered.

"Pretty up there," Clint said, taking another hit.

"Say, I thought we'd go down to the Tamales Cantina and get some dinner," Lenny suggested. "Everyone hungry?"

"I'm starved," Sherry admitted.

"I could eat, too," Lola said.

"Let's go in the VW, do you mind, Lola?" Lenny asked. "That way we can go in one car."

Lola fished out the keys from her purse and handed them to Lenny.

"Wow, Lenny you must be special. Lola won't let anyone drive Betsy, not even me," Sherry said with a grin.

Lenny looked at Lola for confirmation. "Am I special?" He raised his eyebrows in an up and down motion, making everyone laugh.

"I just thought you know the streets better than I do, but yes, you are special." Lola tried not to meet his eyes.

Clint and Sherry piled in the back, sitting very close together out of necessity. Lola climbed in front with Lenny.

As they drove out to the main road Lenny said, "Lola and I used to date in Los Angeles several years ago. We haven't seen each other for ten years. We found out we are still friends, however."

"Have you met Gloria yet?" Clint directed his question to Lola.

"No, she hasn't come by." Lola glanced at Lenny.

"Think she heard you had two beautiful babes visiting you and is mad?" interjected Clint.

"I don't think so. More likely if she heard about Lola and Sherry she'd have been over here in a heartbeat." Lenny said soberly. Maybe he'd better stop that comment. It didn't look like she was rushing right over.

"Are you worried, *amigo?*" Clint asked.

"Maybe a little," Lenny said, "more surprised. She always comes by every two or three days. It's been a week since she's been to my place."

"Oh, so you're counting the days, now." Clint laughed in the back seat.

"Not really. It's just unusual. Maybe she found another guy."

Lola listened intently to the exchange between the two men.

Lenny stopped at the curb next to the Tamales Cantina. They all got out and filed into the *restaurante* which was very crowded, but Clint found them a table in the back.

Lenny and Clint and Sherry ordered chicken tamales, and Lola ordered corn tamales. *Cervezas* were brought immediately to the table with a large bowl of tortilla chips and an extremely hot salsa.

"What have you three been up to?" Clint inquired.

Lola spoke up. "We met *Profesor* Gilberto, Lenny's archaeology teacher. He took us to lunch in the university cafeteria. We visited the Museum of History and the México Revolution Museum and walked all over the gardens outside. And we did some shopping at the street market."

"Sounds like you've seen the sights. Not much more to the town. There are a few jazzy clubs downtown, with some shows. That's about all Chihuahua has to offer. But southwest of here in the mountains there are some fine little villages worth visiting. And of course Copper Canyon, which is spectacular. You have to see that." Clint took a long swig of his *cerveza*.

"We could take a couple of days and head to Creel, the entrance to the Copper Canyon," Lenny said.

Lola looked at Sherry. "That sounds like a good idea."

Sherry nodded.

They finished their dinner, paid the bill and left the *restaurante*.

"That restaurant doesn't serve quite the good food that the one we went to the other night does," Lola said directing her comment to Lenny.

"The Chihuahua Enchilada Restaurante is the best Chihuahua has to offer, I think," he replied.

When they returned to Lenny's, Clint rolled another joint and they sat around the coffee table smoking until Clint said it was time for him to go home.

When Clint stood up to leave he turned to Sherry and said, "Want to go for lunch tomorrow, Sherry? Just you and me?"

Sherry was taken by surprise, but said "Sure," as she stole a glance at Lola.

"You gotta watch Clint, Sherry. He doesn't waste any time with a pretty girl." Lenny said, laughing.

"I'll pick you up around noon," he said on his way out the door. "So long *chica.*"

"I think you have an actual date, Sherry," Lola said, grinning.

"Seriously, Clint is a fast worker, but he's a hell of a good guy. He's got me out of a couple of scrapes."

"Like what?" Lola asked.

"I really don't want to talk about it right now. Don't want to ruin my image," Lenny joked.

"I'm turning in," Sherry said as she headed for the guest room.

"Me too," Lola said following Sherry out of the living room.

Lola felt confused. She still cared for Lenny, but was sure she never needed to act on those feelings. Lenny was becoming less remote. It was possible he would forgive her, in time. And then there was Gloria, with her ever-present non-presence.

≋

Sherry dressed in a pink scoop-necked Mexican blouse and a pair of her newest blue jeans for her lunch with Clint. She painted her toenails and fingernails a soft pink.

Lola came into the bedroom when Sherry was combing her long blond hair. "Wow, you look nice. What do you think of Clint?"

"I don't know yet. He seems nice and he is very attractive, but I don't know him at all." She smiled at Lola.

"Well, he's certainly taken with you, anyone can see that."

Sherry made an O with her lips in the mirror touching up her lipstick.

Lenny came to the doorway. "Clint's here." He gave a lascivious grin in Sherry's direction.

The girls followed Lenny into the living room where Clint was standing just inside the doorway.

"Hey, lady, you look fabulous. I brought some of my primo stuff. Wanna smoke before we eat lunch?"

"Sure. I've never been one to turn down a good offer," Sherry said.

They all laughed at Sherry's high spirits.

Lola and Sherry sat on the couch while Clint lit a joint, propping his cowboy-booted feet on the ottoman.

"Where you going for lunch?" Lenny asked.

"There's a nice little *restaurante* in the Plaza Galeria. Afterwards I thought we'd check out the shops down there."

"Sounds wonderful," Sherry said.

"What are you two going to do while we're gone?" Clint asked, a sparkle in his eye.

"Reckon we'll find something to do." Lenny grinned.

Lola was not entering this conversation. She thought it safer.

"Have fun, you two," she said, as Sherry and Clint left. She watched them climb into Clint's red Corvette and zoom out the drive, kicking up dust as they hurtled down the dirt road.

She turned toward Lenny and saw he was looking at her intently. "What would you like to do? Want to go out to lunch?" he suggested. "We can have our own twosome?"

Lola shook her head. "No, I'll fix us something here. I'd rather just...relax, if you don't mind. I don't think I ever came down from last night when we smoked Clint's weed." Lola smiled as she walked into the kitchen and opened the fridge. When she turned around, Lenny was standing just behind her. His beautiful green eyes were gazing into hers. He put his brown hands on her shoulders and pulled her toward him. Soft lips enveloped hers. She returned his kiss, at first.

Right then she wanted to have sex again with Lenny, but something pulled her back. It was just too fast. She stepped out of his arms. "No, Lenny...I..." Her voice trailed off into silence.

Lenny cupped his hand under her chin. "It's okay. Probably not a good idea." He opened the fridge door wider. "What's for lunch?"

"What do you want?" Lola asked.

"How about a sandwich; peanut butter and banana?"

Lola remembered that was his favorite sandwich. "Coming right up." She tried to sound cheerful to match Lenny's lightness.

The two of them sat down to sandwiches and *cervezas* for lunch. The silence between them continued. Neither had anything to say.

Later, Lola went to her room and lay down on the flowered bed spread, her head resting on her arms. She did not want to resume her affair with Lenny. Inside she knew it would be a mistake right now. She liked him just as much as she had years ago. Discouraging him had its down side. He could turn off to her altogether and ask them to leave. Lola wished his girl friend, Gloria, would show up. That would keep him busy.

In his bedroom Lenny called Gloria's number for the tenth time, but still no answer. It was mighty weird that she hadn't called or dropped by.

⋛⋚

Clint and Sherry parked in the Galeria parking lot and walked to a small *restaurante*. They were given a table next to the front window. As soon as they sat down, five small children appeared outside the window with grubby hands placed on either side of their faces, peering inside. The children were wearing torn and dirty garments, and their faces and hair showed the grime of living on the streets. Behind them were other children with their hands out in hopes of acquiring a few coins.

"Clint, I can't stand this. I have to go out and give them some money." Sherry stood up.

"You stay here, I'll do it," Clint said. "But I have to tell you that within five minutes there will be dozens more outside staring in, as soon as the word gets out."

"I don't care. I can't eat with starving children staring at me."

Clint went outside and dropped a few coins in the children's hands and returned to the table. True to Clint's prediction, in a few minutes several street children appeared at the front window, their grubby little hands splayed palm-flat on the window, their lips pressed to the glass.

Sherry looked away and tried to concentrate on the menu.

Clint ordered his usual, a plate of enchiladas and *una cerveza* and Sherry ordered the same.

"They're hungry. I can't eat with them hungry and watching us." Sherry said. "Look at their little sad eyes."

"Tell you what. I'll go back and talk to the shop owner. I'll arrange for him to give them all meals in the kitchen and pay him for doing that. That will take care of them today but what about tomorrow and next week? We can't afford to feed them indefinitely."

Sherry shook her head, distressed that she didn't have any answers.

When Clint returned, the proprietor was with him. He opened the front door and motioned for all of the children to follow him, speaking to them in Spanish. They raced inside, past him, and headed for the kitchen.

"It looks like they are familiar with this scenario," Sherry said grinning.

"I have no doubt half the tourists that eat in here feed those kids. They are probably better fed than their parents," Clint said

"I didn't realize Chihuahua had a large street population," Sherry reflected.

"There are tons of them. They mostly live near the city dump and spend their days combing through it to find useful items to sell. Some find hanging out at the local *restaurantes* beneficial because many American tourists cannot ignore a hungry child."

Sherry nodded. "Yes, I see what you mean."

Their meals arrived and they sat back to enjoy the tasty flavors when suddenly a shadow was cast over the store window, as maybe two dozen children arrived, chattering and jostling for position as they hugged the window with their palms raised in appeal.

Clint looked at Sherry. "See what I mean? Someone probably said a rich American was eating at the *restaurante* and was giving out money."

Just as quickly as the children arrived, the owner ran out the front door and shooed them all away, then apologized to Clint and Sherry.

Sherry took tentative bites at first. "Clint, there must be something we can do. Can't I find a family and help them — give them some money?" Sherry asked.

"I suppose you could. But do you have the money to help an entire family?"

"Um, yes, I have some money that I don't need. I'd

like to help a family. How would we go about it? I'd like to be able to feed all the children in the barrio."

"Feed them all? Wow, that would be some project. Now feeding one family might be feasible. Let's talk to Lenny when we get back. He might know how to do something like that."

Clint suddenly changed the subject. "Tell me about yourself? Where you grew up — where you lived before you came here."

Sherry laid down her fork. "I grew up in Phoenix, lived there most of my life. A few years ago I moved to the Colorado River area in Arizona, met Lola and we became fast friends."

"How did the two of you meet?"

Sherry looked away. "We met in a bar where she was bartending; she helped me get out of an unhealthy relationship, and eventually I helped her do the same thing."

"So you two have some history together?" Clint said.

Sherry nodded and resumed eating. "What about you? Where were you from before México?" she asked.

"I grew up in Texas, born on the border, my parents were illegal immigrants, but I was born in the U.S. When I was a teenager they were sent back to México. I stayed in Texas with a friend. I worked odd jobs and eventually began smuggling weed over the border. That was several years ago when it was easier. Now it's crazy to take risks like that anymore."

"So what do you do now to make money?" she asked smiling.

"I sell weed, just to locals here in Chihuahua. I make

enough on each deal to live on. It doesn't take much to live here." He gave her a big grin. "I stashed a lot of cash from when I was doing it big time."

"Don't you ever worry about the police?"

Clint shook his head. "The police rarely arrest a small time dealer like me. They want the big guys. Besides, every month I pay one of the detectives on the squad to leave me alone."

Sherry looked at him with eyes wide. "And they leave you alone?"

"*Sí, señorita*," Clint said with his now familiar grin.

She shook her head. "Guess I'll never get used to the dishonesty in the world."

The waitress brought the check, Clint paid it and they left the *restaurante*. He casually linked his arm through hers as they walked by the shops. They wandered into a few; Sherry bought some fancy soap for her and Lola and some candy for Lenny and Clint. On the way back to the car, they saw the children following a couple preparing to enter a *restaurante*.

"I'm serious, Clint. I do want to find a needy family and give them some money."

"How much money are you thinking you'd like to part with?"

"Maybe a couple hundred — how does that sound?"

Clint whistled. "That's a lot of money for a slum family. Can't let the word get out about your identify or you'd be ripped off."

"Do you think Lenny will know how to get in touch with a family?"

"We'll ask him when we get back. He's as likely as anyone to know."

The two of them walked to Clint's Corvette and drove back to Lenny's place. They were both silent on the ride back. Sherry was thinking how much she liked Clint and his easy way with everything he came in contact with. Clint was thinking how beautiful Sherry looked, what great tits she had, and how sweet that she was so compassionate about the hungry children.

⋙⋘

*T*hree days later, Lenny, Lola, Sherry and Clint drove down to the city dump. They parked a block away and walked through the *barrio*. The other people on the street looked like homeless people look everywhere in the world. Their clothes were worn and dirty, the children's hair was tangled and unwashed and most everyone was barefoot. Barely interested in their surroundings, the people gazed blankly ahead of them. The children's eyes were the saddest. Running sores and eyelashes matted shut were visible on many of the children. Lola cringed at their deplorable conditions.

All around the outside of the dump were narrow passages where tar-paper shacks and huts built out of cardboard, canvas, packing crates, whatever material could be scrounged up, were slapped together against the hillside. The scents and smells that prevailed were part garbage-pit and part toilet-sewer. Small alleyways reeked of spoiled meat and fecal matter, with an overpowering stench of urine. The local inhabitants used the alleys as their toilets.

Many of them sat in front of their shacks; the women hollow-eyed and wan. Open sores were visible on their skin. When they saw the *gringos*, hands were automatically stuck out, palms up. There were women with small babies and toddlers. One woman was sitting in front of her hovel, rocking a child in her lap back and forth, as if she were in a rocking chair. She did not have her hand out. Sherry stopped in front of her. The abode behind the woman was made of cardboard. Four more children spilled out from between two pieces.

"This is the one," Sherry said as she turned toward Lenny. Sherry thought she recognized one of the little girls from the *restaurante* where she and Clint had eaten. She wore the same faded blue dress that Sherry had noticed before. Lenny told the girls to give the woman the money inside.

"*Por favor, señora,* may we come inside your house?" Lola asked in Spanish. The woman set the child aside and crawled inside her hovel gesturing for them to follow. She had long dark hair tied up by a string. Her skin was the color of a cashew nut. A ragged blouse hung from her slim shoulders. Barefoot, she crouched on the dirt floor with her five children huddled around her shoulders. The woman was of child-bearing age, obviously, but neither of the girls could tell her age. Lola and Sherry had to bend down, the roof was so low. Lenny and Clint waited outside.

"*Por favor, aprovechese de éste regalo,*" (Please take this gift) Lola said.

Sherry took a pouch from her pocket and handed it to the woman.

The woman looked up at the *gringos* fearfully, but took the pouch from Sherry's outstretched hand. She opened it and took out a large wad of small denomination American money. Her eyes opened wide in amazement. She looked quickly at Lola and Sherry and snatched the money from the pouch, slipping it inside her blouse, as if she were expecting them to take back the money.

"*Hasta la vista*," Lola said as she and Sherry left the hovel.

The four of them made a fast retreat back through the twisting alleys that wound around the perimeter of the dump. They passed a man who was either inebriated or sick, vomiting against the wall. When they got back to the Volkswagen, they all crawled inside and drove away quickly.

≋≋

*L*enny had confided in Clint his concern that Gloria had disappeared.

"I know a guy that owns a nightclub downtown," Clint said. "I'll ask him if he has heard anything about Gloria. There's a network that exists among the dancers down there and he may have heard if she quit her job in the stage show and left town."

Two days later, Clint came by Lenny's place. "I made contact with the nightclub owner and he says he has some info on Gloria but he wants to meet with you and give it to you. I can arrange a meeting if you want."

"Yeah, do it," Lenny said. Lola came into the kitchen just as Clint was telling Lenny. "I would like to go along with you. Okay?"

Lenny hesitated. Then, "I suppose it's okay," he answered. "What do you think, Clint?"

"I don't see a problem."

The meeting was set up for the next afternoon. Lola and Lenny followed Clint's Corvette to an old warehouse. Clint disappeared inside and Lenny and Lola were told to wait. In a few minutes Clint appeared at the door and waved them in. They got out of the truck and walked to the building. Half of the roof was caved in, several windows broken out, and the big bay door was off the hinges.

When the two of them came abreast of Clint, he told them to follow him. They entered the warehouse and followed him down a long corridor. Lola, wrinkling her nose at the smell of mildew, decaying garbage, and decades of dust, stifled a sneeze. Clint opened a door at the end of the corridor.

Lola had a bad feeling. She had an urge to run, to get out of there. She usually trusted her instincts but this time she stuffed it down. Lenny wanted to find out what had happened to Gloria and he was determined to go to the meeting.

They entered the room and saw a very fat man sitting at a desk under the window. He was dressed in business clothes, wearing a brown double-breasted suit and a dark fedora on his head.

"Sit down," the fat man said. The room stunk of mildew and cigar smoke.

After the two were seated, Clint introduced the man behind the desk. "This is Juan Bolero. He owns the Dolores Cantina downtown. He can help you find Gloria."

"*Cómo está?*" Juan asked.

"*Bien*," Lenny answered.

"You can leave now, Clint," Juan said. Clint hesitated, and then left the room.

Juan Bolero glanced at Lenny but seemed more interested in Lola. He looked her up and down, smiling, his gold inlays gleaming between his lips. "Do you want a job dancing in my night club?" he said. "What is your name, *señorita?*"

"*Lupe*, and no," Lola answered.

"*Lupe* what?" he asked.

"Never mind what her name is, we're here to find Gloria Bernabe," Lenny said.

Juan picked up his cigar that was resting in the ash tray and took a puff. He looked at Lenny over the end of his cigar. "Your name is Lenny, correct? Gloria is your girlfriend?"

Lenny nodded.

"I happen to know where Gloria is." He looked down at the photo on his desk. "Is this Gloria?" He handed it to Lenny and Lola.

Lenny nodded.

Lola saw a picture of an attractive, olive skinned woman, with long dark hair. She experienced a jolt of déjà vu. It was like looking into a mirror! My God! That picture looks like me, was her first thought. She turned to Lenny. "You didn't tell me she looked like me."

Lenny shrugged, looking down at the photo. "I guess I hadn't thought about that until just now. You two do resemble each other."

She looked at Lenny strangely. How had he not noticed it? It was so obvious.

Juan took back the picture. He laid it on top of another photo. Lola got a glimpse of the other photo. It was a picture of her! She couldn't understand why this man had a photo of her. A professional photo that she'd had made in Las Vegas!

"It will cost you to find her," the fat man said.

"How much?"

"A grand," Juan said with a smile.

Lenny laughed. "What? I don't have that kind of money. And if I did, I wouldn't pay you that outrageous price to find Gloria. You can have her." Lenny stood up, ready to leave.

"Sit down," Juan ordered.

Lola stood also and she and Lenny defiantly headed for the door. Just as they reached it, two men bolted through the doorway and grabbed both of them by the arms. Lola struggled and Lenny tried to get his hands free. She kicked the guy holding her in the nuts. He howled and let go. She ran through the door and darted down the hallway. When she'd gone a few paces, she could hear them beating Lenny. Stopping, she turned around and went back through the open door.

One of the henchmen had socked Lenny in the nose and it was bleeding. He was kicking him in the ribs when Lola came back into the room.

"Stop," she said.

Juan was standing behind the desk, his cigar clenched between his teeth. He gestured with his hand for his men to stop beating Lenny. "You are quite a little spitfire, aren't you Lola?"

Both Lenny and Lola looked at him. "How did you know my name?" she asked.

"Oh, I know your name and I'm going to hold you here for a while until a certain person from Las Vegas gets here and takes you off my hands."

Lola was stunned! My God, they had found her here!

By this time the man who was squirming on the floor had recovered enough to stand up and grab Lola again, holding her so she couldn't reach his crotch with her feet.

The two henchmen walked them out of the room and down the hallway to another room. The shorter of the two opened a door with a key and tossed Lola inside, slamming the door and locking it. She stayed on her feet, but came up short against a cot on the opposite side of the tiny room. The sound of a struggle in the next room told her they were holding Lenny there. Then the jangle of the key in the lock and she heard them walk away down the hall.

The only good thing about this terrible situation was that Lenny was locked in just next door. And Clint

— Where was he? Was he in on this? Would he have betrayed her to this man, perhaps for money? But he didn't know about Vegas and that the Mob was looking for her. They could have shown him a picture of her and asked him if he had seen her. Clint had some explaining to do — if they ever saw him again.

The more she thought about it, the angrier she became. Why did Lenny not tell her that Gloria looked enough like her to be her sister? He had put her in danger here. He let her come along, knowing she looked like Gloria.

She waited calmly for what seemed like ten or fifteen minutes until she could no longer hear any voices or noises outside the room. Quietly she knocked on the wall between the rooms. Lenny knocked back. She spoke softly to the wall. "Can you hear me?" No response. He couldn't hear. She went over and lay down on the cot. A filthy army blanket on top of the mattress scratched her arms. Maybe she could have outrun them when she kicked the guy, but she couldn't leave Lenny there. They were in deep shit because of her. Apparently the Mob had connections with Juan and had tracked her down here to Chihuahua. She realized for the first time that Gloria had been mistaken for her, and probably was not alive. Had Lenny come to this conclusion too?

She was overcome by the realization that the Mob was still hunting her. How had they tracked her to Chihuahua?

She had to do something. Staying here was not an option. When the Las Vegas people arrived they would kill her and maybe Lenny, too. She was staring at the ceiling when she became aware of the grate above her head approximately twenty inches square. Across the room was a wooden chair. Dragging it over, she placed it on the cot. Standing on it was no small feat; she had to hold onto the wall to keep from toppling off the chair. Reaching the grate with one hand, she pushed on it. The edges were sharp and she scraped the side of her fingers, but it lifted easily. However, there was no way she could climb through. There was too much distance between her and the opening to be able to pull up and through it. Taking inventory of the room, she saw a table in one corner. Climbing down, she moved the cot as quietly as she could, and pulled the table in place under the grate, placed the chair on top of the table and began her climb carefully up the tier. This time when she tried to stand up she had to crouch. Reaching the grate, she pushed it upward and slid it to one side. The ventilation duct beyond was big enough for her to crawl toward the room next door, however she couldn't get through the opening. Tearing at the ceiling tile two of them came loose. She grabbed them before they fell to the floor and tossed them on the cot. Dust and debris floated down and she felt a sneeze coming on. At last she could stand up with her head and upper body inside the air duct. Pulling herself up, she angled her body toward the room Lenny was in. Lying down in the duct she began to crawl. Edging her way along, crawling marine-combat style, she pulled the cover off the grate into the room Lenny was in, and slid it aside. Lenny was lying on the floor looking up at the ceiling.

"My God, Lola, I heard you and thought it was a pretty big rat up there." He jumped up and began sliding a small table under the opening.

"We have to see where this leads. This is our only way." She spoke softly.

With one thrust Lenny tore away some tiles, and pulled himself inside the grate opening and into the duct passage. Lola had crawled down the duct and was heading away from the rooms in which they were imprisoned. She could see a light at the end in the distance. It was a very tight fit for Lenny but Lola made good time. When she reached the light, she could see the end of the duct opening onto the roof. Scrambling over rough edges she squatted, waiting for him to join her. Finally his head and arms appeared and she moved back so he could get out. The roof was flat, so there was no problem keeping their footing.

Lenny put his finger to his lips, and motioned for her to follow him. He headed for the far edge where they had parked his truck. Sure enough, when he leaned over the edge, his truck was still where he'd parked it. He touched the keys in his pocket. Lucky for them, they hadn't searched him.

They crept along the roof until they came to a ladder. It was pretty rickety and when Lenny put his foot on the first rung it wobbled. Voices wafted up from below as they continued as quietly as they could down the ladder. Lenny went down first and then Lola followed. Reaching the ground Lenny pulled Lola back into the shadows. The men's laughter seemed to be coming from around the end of the warehouse. He took Lola's hand and they stealthily moved toward the truck. Both went to the driver's door and Lola crawled under the steering wheel to the passenger's side. Lenny slid behind the wheel, placed the key in the ignition, turned the engine over and drove like hell out of the parking area. They could hear shouts behind them, but Lenny was down the road and onto a main thoroughfare, taking the first exit. He back-tracked and got back on the freeway going in the opposite direction.

She looked at Lenny. "Why didn't you tell me I looked like Gloria? And you let me come along knowing they would connect us?" The more she said, the madder she got.

He glanced sideways at Lola. "I didn't really think about it. Gloria is Gloria and you are you. I didn't think the two of you looked alike until you mentioned it."

"I think that's some kind of bullshit, Lenny. Only an imbecile wouldn't see the resemblance."

Lenny was quiet.

"I just want you to know I'm really steamed about this. You put me in jeopardy bringing me along."

"You wanted to come."

"If I'd known I looked like Gloria maybe I wouldn't have."

Lenny glanced at her. "I'm sorry, Lola."

Lola let out her breath in a long sigh. "I really thought we were goners," she said, looking at Lenny's profile.

"I wouldn't ever put you in danger on purpose, don't you know that?" Lenny said.

Lola was silent.

Trying for a response from her, he said, "That was pretty smart of you. How did you know to do that?" He turned his head quickly and smiled at her for a second before turning his attention back to the road.

"I think I saw it in a movie once. How the good guy got out of a locked room."

Lenny placed his right hand over her left which was lying in her lap. "You were really great. I'm sorry."

Lola nodded, accepting his apology. "Lenny. The Mob has tracked me here — Juan probably knows where you live — What will we do? — Sherry is waiting for us there — she's in danger — our money is locked up — We're in an awful mess." Her words came in short gasps.

"Don't worry, we'll figure out what to do next. First I need to find a safe place to stop so we can talk."

"I really thought they wouldn't find me in México."

"Don't worry, Lola, we'll work this out. We can't go to the police because they are often in the pocket of the drug dealers and the crooks. It looks like we're on our own."

"Say, what about your friend Clint? He led us into that trap. Think he was in on it?"

"Somehow I don't think he knew what Juan was really after. He thought he was helping me find Gloria."

"How long have you known him?" Lola asked.

"Ever since I moved here ten years ago. He's been my weed connection all that time. Never once did he take advantage of me." Lenny pulled off the Avenida Juan Paola, down a side street and into a gated exit to a garage, and parked.

"Could we go to Clint's? I have some questions I want to ask him."

"Yeah, we could drive over there and let Clint know what happened. But I'm pretty sure he didn't mean to get us in that bind."

Lenny looked at Lola. She had dirt on her nose, her hair was tangled and her gold earrings glistened in the sun. He slid over toward her, put his right arm around her shoulder and kissed her on the lips.

Lola was taken by surprise. Her sudden anger disappeared. She easily gave in to the remembered pleasure.

When Lenny pulled back he said, "That was for saving our butts back there."

Lola didn't feel there was anything necessary to say, but she was acutely aware of her heart beating faster. The scent of sweat and Lenny's maleness hung over him like a hormone cloud. She remembered the smell of him and how much it used to turn her on. Lenny turned back to the wheel and backed out of the exit way.

"I'm heading for Clint's, and we need to get Sherry out of my house."

⋛⋚

Clint was drinking a *cerveza* when Lenny pulled up in his drive. He came to the door immediately. "Did you find Gloria?" he asked.

"No, we didn't. Juan threw us into locked rooms. He said he was holding us until someone came from Vegas to pick me up." Lola said with a touch of anger.

"Wha-a-at?" Clint responded in surprise.

Lenny was silent, while Lola explained briefly about her being a witness to a murder in Vegas over a year ago and how one hit man already had been killed in Arizona after he found her. And now another was on her trail. "I want to know if you knew Juan was looking for me when you took us there," Lola asked Clint point-blank.

Clint gazed at Lola in amazement. "Of course not! I wouldn't do anything like that to my friends. I didn't know anyone was looking for you. I asked Juan about Gloria and he said he wanted to talk to Lenny personally."

Lenny interrupted the conversation. "I knew this, Clint. I told Lola I was sure you didn't lead us there knowing Juan was looking for her."

Lola's attitude softened. "I'm sorry Clint. I had to be sure. Sherry is at the house and we need to get her out. Also we've stashed our money in Lenny' safe. We need to get that before we can move on."

Lenny looked at Lola. "What do you mean — move on? You don't need to go. We'll find a place to hide out until this thing gets resolved or goes away."

"It's not going away, Lenny." Lola said with sadness in her voice. "A few days ago you said we could stay a few days. The few days are up."

"That was then. This is now," Lenny said.

She turned to Clint. "Why didn't you tell me that Gloria and I looked alike?"

Clint looked from Lenny to Lola. "I guess I thought Lenny did."

Lola shook her head. "Lenny didn't even notice the resemblance until I saw a picture of her on top of one of my Vegas promotional photos and pointed it out."

"You mean Juan thought Gloria was you?" Clint asked.

"That's what I think," Lola replied.

"It really didn't register that the two of them looked so much alike until Lola pointed it out," Lenny said, somewhat chagrined.

Clint changed the subject. "I've been thinking. I know a place we can stay for a while. My Uncle Diego has a small cottage in Los Campos about an hour from Chihuahua."

"I have to get Sherry out of your place, Lenny," Lola said. "Will you help me?"

"Of course." He put his arm around Lola's shoulders.

"I'll go get Sherry and meet you two in Los Campos," Clint offered.

Lenny looked at Clint for a second. "Okay, pal. We'd appreciate it. But we need to do it now. I'll have to go back for the money later. They won't find it. It's well hidden. I only hope Juan hasn't decided to go to my place before you get there."

Clint got up, took his shotgun from the rack on the wall. "I'm on my way. Meet me at the *mercado* in Los Campos and we'll go out to my uncle's place from there."

Lenny handed his keys to Clint. "Take my truck. It travels the trail into the back of my property better than your Corvette."

Clint handed his Corvette keys to Lenny. "See you in a couple of hours in Los Campos."

He was out the door and into the truck and down the road before Lola had stood up.

⋛⋚

*S*herry was smoking a joint, sipping a *cerveza* and painting her nails. The radio was on, playing some *Norteno Mexicano* music. Her hair was wrapped in a towel, still wet from the shower.

Where were Lola and Lenny? They had been gone a long time and she was getting a little worried. Clint had told them to follow him to a warehouse. They all three had insisted she stay at Lenny's. Damn, she was missing all the action. Maybe they had found Gloria and Lenny was wishing they hadn't. Sherry could tell Lenny was falling for Lola again. And she thought she detected the same from Lola. As for her, she was really taken with Clint, but she wouldn't sleep with him, yet. It was just too soon. Not that she didn't want to. But she still remembered Ronnie, and felt she might be betraying their love by taking a lover so soon. She had never felt about another man the way she had Ronnie. They were just getting to know each other and were deeply in love when the train wreck in Arizona, with Ronnie as the engineer, took his life. No use crying over the past; she would tell Clint about Ronnie later.

Her nails dry, she combed her fine, blond hair, pulling it back in a pony tail. She put on some clean jeans and a tee-shirt, went to the kitchen and ate some chips and salsa with the last of her beer.

She was looking out the back yard at the chickens free ranging when Clint suddenly appeared around the end of the chicken coop on the run, with a shotgun in his hand. He hopped up the steps of the porch and opened the kitchen door while Sherry stood with her mouth open.

"Hi. Get your purse, grab a couple of changes of clothes, and come with me." He put his hand on her arm and walked her to the guest room where she and Lola had been bunking.

"Throw in a change of clothes for Lola, too. Hurry!" His voice was low and urgent, his face tight with tension, creased lines across his brow.

"What's happening? Is Lola all right?"

"Yes, she's fine. Do what I say, *pronto*."

Sherry felt strangely scattered but managed to grab two changes of clothing for her and Lola, threw them in a satchel, and picked up her purse.

"What about our money?" she said.

"Lenny said we'd have to come back for it later. We have no time to spare right now. Come on." Clint said.

They made their way back to the kitchen, ducked out the back door and started for the chicken coop behind which Clint had parked Lenny's truck.

"I didn't see you drive in," Sherry said. Clint still had his hand on Sherry's arm and was ushering her toward the vehicle.

He pointed toward the road down by the highway.

Where the dirt road began a cloud of dust rose on the breeze as a car sped toward the ranch.

"Hurry, get in."

Sherry slipped into the truck, and Clint backed up and turned around, heading out the other side of the ranch. This was a mere wagon trail, with lots of rocks and sand traps which slowed down their progress. Eventually he reached a gravel road and could drive at a faster pace away from Lenny's house. Sherry could no longer see the vehicle that was headed for Lenny's place.

"Tell me what happened." Sherry insisted.

Clint told her what Lenny and Lola had told him when they arrived at his place. "Lenny asked me to come and get you and we are to meet them at my uncle Diego's place in Los Campos."

"You mean the Mob from Vegas is hunting Lola down here in México?" A glint of fear appeared in her eyes.

Clint nodded. "We think so. They found her thanks to that dick-head, Juan. He tricked me into thinking he would help Lenny find Gloria."

"Did you find Gloria?"

"Nope. But Gloria is a dead ringer for Lola, forgive the pun."

"What do you mean?"

Lenny explained the resemblance between the two women. "And Gloria could turn up dead."

"How come Lenny didn't tell us that Gloria resembled Lola?"

"Apparently he wasn't that aware of it until it was pointed out to him."

"Wait a minute. Gloria and Lola look alike and Lenny didn't say anything?"

Clint glanced at Sherry. "He must have been in denial about it. Can't think of any other reason, can you?"

Sherry shook her head and sat in silent contemplation, wondering if Lola would ever be free of the Vegas Mob. It shouldn't still be an albatross around her neck. Lola was strong, independent and beautiful. She didn't deserve all this trauma and headache with her life in danger.

"So we're going to your uncle's place?" Sherry stole a sideways look at Clint.

He nodded.

"Will Lola and Lenny be there, or are you taking me off to have your way with me?"

He nodded again. "I said we were meeting them there, didn't I?" He glanced over at her, saw her smile and knew she was kidding him.

"Damn, woman. Don't josh me like that. I wouldn't do anything to you against your will." By this time, Clint was smiling too. "Of course, if you were to twist my arm, I might be convinced to kiss you a whole lot."

Sherry smiled but chose to ignore his comment. "I need to get serious for a minute, Clint. I'm worried about Lola. How we can keep her alive and the rest of us too, for that matter?"

"It's okay, girl, I understand. I'm kind of worried myself how we four are going to get out of this jam. When we get to Los Campos we'll sit down with Lenny and Lola and have a pow-wow."

"How far is it?"

"An hour away."

Sherry sat back and closed her eyes, resting her head against the back of the seat. It seemed like she and Lola had had a few weeks of fun and relaxation traveling to México, reuniting with an old friend and meeting new ones and now it was starting all over again; the fear, the hiding, and the running. What would become of them? When would Lola be free of the Las Vegas Mob?

≳≲

*G*uido looked down at the photo of Lola Raines. Damn, she was a hard woman to kill! He'd just had a phone call from his connection in Chihuahua, México, Juan Bolero. Guido had been told that Jack 'hit' the wrong woman!

He pressed the button on his desk for his secretary. "Cindy, get Jack on the phone right now."

In a few minutes the phone rang. Guido picked up the receiver.

"Jack. You 'hit' the wrong woman. What the hell's the matter with you? I give you a simple assignment and you fuck it up."

Guido listened for a few seconds. "I don't give a shit that she looked like the mark. You get back down there and find this Raines-Morales woman and get rid of her once and for all. You got that? And Jack…this trip is on your nickel. You've already been paid for getting rid of her." Guido slammed the receiver down.

What's the world coming to when you can't count on your hit men to get rid of problems? This Lola dame had been a thorn in his side since last year. He wasn't sure if she was even at Tony Ricco's house the night his men killed him, but to make it a clean job, since she was Tony's girlfriend, he had to 'do' her, too.

Guido went to the bar, poured himself a half glass of Glenfiddich over ice, cut the end from a Cuban cigar and lit it with his 18-carat gold cigarette lighter. Retiring to his favorite chair, he leaned back and looked out the ceiling-to-floor windows of his penthouse office at the spectacular night lights that spread across the Strip in Las Vegas.

Maybe it was time to retire Jack Marchetti. He and Martin had failed to kill Lola in Mohave Valley last year. And now this fuck-up; killing the wrong woman. He'd think on this a while.

≋

*T*he four of them sat around the circular dining table at Clint's uncle's cottage. Four cups of coffee, a pack of cigarettes and chips and salsa were on the table.

"So here's what we know so far," Lenny's voice was strong. "The Vegas Mob wants Lola dead and has sent out another hit man. We saw a picture on Juan's desk of Lola. The Mob probably contacted several connections in different Méxican cities and hit the jackpot in Chihuahua. Juan Bolero saw Lola's picture and fingered Gloria as Lola. Someone came down from Vegas and probably did away with her," Lenny's voice became soft at this point. "Or maybe she is being held somewhere. When Juan saw Lola in the flesh, he realized his mistake and decided to hold her until he notified the people in Vegas. We need to get Lola and Sherry's money hidden in my house, and escape Juan and the Vegas people."

Clint looked at Sherry and Lola with raised eyebrows. "Not as easy as it sounds. How much money is in Lenny's house?"

"I think you can trust Clint, after he got Sherry out of the house in the nick of time," Lenny added.

"Lola and I each have approximately 10,000 American dollars in mostly $100 bills, give or take a few hundred," Sherry explained.

Clint whistled. "No wonder you could give that slum family $200. Where'd you get a bundle like that?" He was looking at Sherry.

"A dear friend passed away and left it to Lola and me," she said.

"I'm thinking Clint and I should go back at night and get the money. Maybe they won't be watching the place once they see we've gone."

"It's too risky right now, Lenny," Lola protested.

"Yeah, we can do that Lenny," Clint agreed, ignoring Lola's concerns. "Maybe wait a couple of nights and then go in around 3 a.m."

"I was thinking the same thing," Lenny agreed.

The four of them sat in silence for awhile, contemplating the situation.

Sherry's voice was faint. "What are we going to do about the hit man?"

"We'll be on our guard at all times. Clint and I will be armed; we figure the best way to deal with this situation is to fight back." Lenny looked at Lola while this information sunk in. "Lola, would you and Sherry pick up some food if we drop you in town? Clint and I have some special shopping to do in preparation for our uninvited visitor. We might as well plan on being here for a few days or even weeks. That's okay with your uncle, Clint?"

Clint nodded. "He rarely comes up here anymore. He says he's getting too old to hike in the canyons."

"Thanks so much, Clint, for offering us this refuge," Lola said. "I don't know what Sherry and I would do if we didn't have a place to hide." She looked from one to the other. "I'm real sorry I got you three into this jam. I feel like I should move on. Not endanger you anymore."

Lenny put his arm around Lola. "I want you to stay right here. I'm not about to let anything happen to you. Clint and I can protect you and Sherry."

Lola turned to Sherry. "What do you think?"

"I think we should stay. We have two strong men on our side. There are four of us now. We won't let them get us." She smiled at Clint, Lenny and Lola.

"I think that settles it then," Lenny said.

The four of them piled into Lenny's truck and headed into Los Campos, Sherry and Lola crammed into the tiny cab behind the driver's seat.

⧖

*T*he garbage truck backed out on the edge of the dump and began lowering the truck bed. A muscular man with wide shoulders jumped out from behind the wheel and watched the refuse fall over the cliff. Something large was stuck between two boxes. He reached in to separate the tie-up and grabbed hold of something hard and cold. It felt like the leg of an animal. He pulled it free and saw then that it was an arm of a person. His hand released the object like he was holding a scalding coal; he swore under his breath. The stench that rose from the body made the truck driver want to throw up. He pulled the lever to stop the movement of the debris.

"*Dios mio*," he whispered. "*Otro muerto.*" (Another dead body.) The man sometimes found corpses in the garbage, but he never got used to it. He got into the truck and drove a short way to the office.

Inside the dilapidated office a man with greasy hands and a cowboy hat on his head sat behind a table. "*Que paso?*" the man asked.

The garbage truck driver explained his cargo. The man behind the desk got up and went out to inspect the back of the truck. He climbed inside and moved a box out of the way. The woman was in her twenties, with long raven hair, wearing a blue blouse and blue jeans. Her eyes were open and she had a large gash across her throat.

He jumped down and cursed. He went to the

phone, picked up the receiver and placed a call to the *Departemento Del Policia*.

※※

*L*ola and Sherry drove into the small town of Los Campos, to pick up bread and milk. Lola spied the newspaper stand next to the door. On the front page of the *Chihuahua Registro*, in Spanish, was an article about the latest body found at the city dump. Lola scanned it quickly then translated it for Sherry. The body had been identified as Gloria Bernabe.

"Damn it!" Lola said. "Lenny will be sad. He figured she was probably dead, but this confirms it." Lola took the paper to the counter and paid for it. The girls went out to Lenny's truck and started back to Diego's place.

"They killed her, Lola. We've got to get away from here," Sherry said, as if the full realization of the danger had just sunk in.

Lola nodded, but was silent. Would she ever be safe? What must she do to get away from these people? She had never gone to the police, and she never intended to. She wasn't really a threat to the Mob. If only they realized that.

Pulling into the back yard of Diego's, the girls entered the house by the back door. Clint and Lenny were cleaning the two .45 caliber handguns that they'd purchased a few days before. Lenny was holding the gun up to the light and sighting down the barrel when the screen door banged behind the girls. Lola placed the paper in front of him on the table and put her hand on his shoulders.

Lenny could read some Spanish, enough to understand the article. He was silent as he reached up and patted Lola's hand. He turned to Clint. "Tonight's the night. We go back to my house and get the money."

"Right," Clint agreed.

Lola removed her hand from underneath Lenny's. "I need to leave. You three are in enough trouble. If I'm gone, they'll leave you alone."

"Listen, honey," Lenny said. "You came here to visit me and expected a safe haven. I'm not letting those bastards run you off. We're in this together, you and me. I've got a score to settle with them now that they've killed Gloria." He turned to Clint. "You don't need to be mixed up with us any longer. Lola and I will leave here."

"Wait a minute," Sherry said. "No one asked me how I feel. I threw in with Lola in Arizona. I'm in this to the end. She's my best friend. I don't intend to abandon her now."

"Likewise. I'm in, too," Clint said, with a big grin. "I don't like anyone pushing me or my friends around. And Gloria was my friend, too. And now, so is Lola."

"Well, honey. Looks like you still have us three for sidekicks whether you like it or not."

Lola had tears in her eyes. She swallowed the lump in her throat. "Thanks everyone. I really appreciate your friendship."

Lenny put his arm around her shoulders and pulled

her into an embrace. A few seconds later he let her go.

"Tonight," Lenny said. "Clint and I will go into Chihuahua about 3:30 a.m. We should be back here by dawn."

"Why don't Sherry and I go with you? We can help."

"Absolutely not! I don't want you anywhere near Juan's people."

"Lenny. Will you drive Betsy back here? I can't leave her there." Lola was referring to her VW Beetle.

"I'll try. If all goes well, I'll bring her back."

Sherry went to the fridge and started preparing a simple evening meal. Lola got up and helped. Lenny and Clint continued to clean and load the .45 pistols.

>≶

*L*enny and Clint headed back to Chihuahua in the early morning hours. Lola got up to make a thermos of coffee for them. The last thing Lenny did was pull her to him and kiss her on the mouth.

On the ride to his ranch he thought about his feelings for Lola. He realized now he had never really fallen out of love with her. She had hurt him all those years ago by leaving him, but this was another time and perhaps he had a second chance. He wondered about his obvious denial regarding the resemblance between Gloria and Lola. How had he not admitted to himself that he was attracted right from the beginning to Gloria because she reminded him of Lola? Not just her looks. She had the same wild, untamed streak in her. It was a shame that Gloria was murdered because of the physical resemblance to Lola. Nothing he could do about that now. The main thing he must do is protect Lola.

The miles had gone by quickly; they were approaching Lenny's property. Clint poured two coffees in tin cups and handed one to Lenny. "Think we'll have a welcoming committee when we arrive at your place?"

"Could be. We'll park the truck about a half mile from the house in back and walk in. Best to surprise anyone that might be on guard."

Once they got off the main road and onto the trail that ran through Lenny's property, he slowed and turned off the headlights. The moon was full and gave enough light to see the ruts in the ground. He pulled up under a tree, and stopped. With the engine turned off, they could hear the desert night sounds. A lone coyote called across the prairie. Soon they heard a mournful answer. The moon outlined the rock outcroppings next to the tree. This was a good shelter for the truck; not easily seen at a distance. Up ahead they could see the vague shape of the house and outbuildings in the moonlight.

It took Lenny and Clint about ten minutes to walk to the chicken coop. Lenny hadn't planned it, but Betsy, Lola's VW, was parked behind the coop, a straight shot to the back trail and the truck. Cautiously they crept along the edge of the yard until they reached the back porch. Lenny laid his finger to his lips and motioned for Clint to wait for him. He made his way around the house to the side. An old truck stood in the driveway. There *was* someone inside.

Lenny made his way back to Clint and motioned for him to follow. Around one side of the house there was a window that Lenny had left unlocked. Jasmine blossoms from the bush fell around their shoulders as they crawled inside.

They were in the girls' bedroom. Clothes were strewn on the floor and the bedclothes were tangled in a ball. They crept to the door and Lenny slowly opened it. He and Clint quietly moved toward the living room. At the doorway, Lenny saw a stranger asleep on the couch. The stranger's gun was holstered on his hip and he still wore his boots. Lenny stepped over to the couch, drew his .45 from his belt and leveled it at the man asleep. He poked him on the shoulder with the butt of the gun. "Get up," he said.

The man woke with a start and reached for his gun. Then he saw the .45 pistol staring him in the face. He froze.

"Stand up," Lenny said. Clint took the man's gun, carefully placing it in his pocket. The man got off the couch and stood. He looked like one of the men that had locked him and Lola up in the warehouse.

Clint covered the man with his gun. He produced a coil of rope and the two of them proceeded to tie the stranger to a straight-backed chair.

"*Por favor*," he sputtered. "Don't tie me up. I just stumbled into an empty house for the night," he said in Spanish.

"Who sent you here?" Lenny asked, although he didn't expect an answer.

"No one," the man said.

Lenny pulled a handkerchief from his pocket and stuffed it into the stranger's mouth.

The room had drawers pulled out and pillows cut with their stuffing hanging out. A quick walk into the kitchen showed the same disarray, as if a dirt-devil from the desert had entered the house. Flour was spilled on the floor, the pantry was open and dried beans were scattered across the tiles. Lenny wondered what they were looking for. Money? Why had the house been so furiously searched?

"Find the girls' suitcases and throw everything that looks like their clothing into them," Lenny instructed Clint.

Lenny went to his bedroom. His room was in a shambles too, but when he opened the closet door, no one had discovered the panel to the safe. He opened it quickly, removed Lola and Sherry's money, and all of his own. He put the cash in two pillowcases, separating his money from the girls. Shutting the safe and the paneled door, he threw some clothes into a small gym bag for himself. Finding his tooth brush and shaving gear, he tossed that in too. Returning to the guest room, he saw that Clint had finished filling the suitcases.

"Let's get out of here," Lenny said. They carried the suitcases out the back door and headed for the VW.

On the way, Lenny and Clint ducked into the chicken coop and scattered some grain on the floor for the sleeping chickens. Lenny grabbed a basket and filled it with eggs. Then they climbed into Betsy and drove to the truck. Clint jumped out, got into the truck and led the way down the trail to the paved road.

Clint lit a cigarette as he pulled onto the main road. Wow, he'd been in such a rut for years, he didn't realize how a little adventure could kick up the adrenaline. He felt tingling sensations all along his neck and spine. His breath came faster; and he noticed he was more alive than he had been in years.

He thought of his time growing up in Brownsville, a border town in Texas. He had missed his parents at first when they got shipped back to México, but then he got involved in school activities, and he liked living with his friends, the Martinez's. They were naturalized citizens and also friends of his parents, and they took Clint in so he had a place to live. Dealing weed after he left high school became his occupation. When Edgar Martinez found out he told him to move out. Clint did, and eventually started moving weed from across the border into Texas. After ten years it became too risky; the DEA was cracking down on dealers, so he quit. He decided to move down to Chihuahua because the girl he was going with at the time was from there. When they broke up, Clint stayed and, although he didn't need the money, he found a job in a cowboy clothing store, which suited him as he dressed in boots, Stetson and jeans. After Clint had worked there a few years, the owner sold the business. He began living on his savings, which were considerable—his illicit drug money. Clint shook his head at the memories; marijuana was all he'd sold, but he'd had plenty of opportunity to sell other drugs. He didn't think marijuana was harmful; however, cocaine, methamphetamine and opium were all destructive. Some of his friends had been taken down by these drugs.

Now Sherry had come into his life. He was very attracted to her, but so far they hadn't slept together. He didn't want to rush her. With this Vegas Mob thing hanging over Lola's head, he knew Sherry was very worried about her friend. Actually all four of them were in danger. Since he and Lenny had made Lola's predicament their business, they were all in the line of fire.

He had no plans beyond the moment and staying in his Uncle Diego's place for a while. He figured they were as safe there as anywhere. And the more he was around Sherry the better he liked her.

*L*enny could see Clint in the truck up ahead on the deserted highway. They'd be back in Los Campos in less than an hour.

He remembered back to the time when he first met Lola in West Los Angeles in the Laundromat. Sheba had been alive then, his loyal German shepherd. He and Lola had a wonderful, romantic love affair. It had really hurt him when she broke it off. He tried to resume his life, but he'd really grieved losing her. Then Sheba had died and he had another grieving period to work through. That was when he decided to move to México. A distant relative in México City had helped him buy the property in Chihuahua. Americans couldn't buy property outright without a Méxican citizen also on the bill of sale. To make money he'd done gardening and landscaping for the wealthy during the ten years he'd lived here and that had made a decent living for him.

He thought about his youth growing up in West Los Angeles. His father had been a lawyer and his mother a successful artist. When they had died suddenly in an auto accident, Lenny was fourteen. He was devastated. His maternal grandmother offered him a home and he stayed until he was twenty. He took some classes at UCLA, but his real love was gardening and landscaping, so he finally quit school and got a good-paying job. When his grandmother died, he inherited the house located on a lovely spot on Mulholland Drive in Beverly Hills. Eventually he sold it for a lot of money and invested most of it. He was able to live on the interest the principle generated. The bulk of the money was still tied up in investments and savings in the U.S.

There had been a lot of loss in his life and a lot of grieving. About the time he was getting used to his grandmother being gone from his life he met Lola. It was really love at first sight for him. It had lasted a little over a year. He never understood what Lola was afraid of with their relationship. He did understand that she'd had a difficult time getting close to people because of the abuse she suffered at the hands of her father. That man was a real bastard! He started molesting her when she was twelve. Finally she ran away when she was seventeen after telling her mother that she saw her father pick up the little girl next door to take to a circus.

That's when she told her mother about what her father had done to her all those years. Her mother called her a liar and said to stay out of her father's business. When her mother went to work that night at the local diner, Lola packed a suitcase and left home forever. She told Lenny she never saw her parents again. Her father died in a fire as a volunteer fireman, and her mother died in a sanitarium of cirrhosis of the liver.

Looking back he figured he'd had a pretty good childhood compared to Lola's, in spite of losing the three people he loved most, his parents and his grandmother.

If they could just get out of this jam and manage to stay alive, he might have a second chance with her.

Lenny came out of his reverie when he saw Diego's place just down the road. Lola and Sherry would be glad to get their money back. Another pow-wow was on the agenda to decide what would be their next step.

≳≲

*A*gente de policia Lieutenant Gus Mendez shuffled the papers on his desk. His jet black hair and bronze skin complimented his blue eyes. Standing five feet, five inches tall, Gus Mendez had a look about him that kept most men at a distance. His powerful build with wide shoulders and narrow hips had caught many a *señorita's* eye in his early days. His wife of thirty-five years had passed away five years ago and he now devoted all his time to police work. He was a diligent and honest policeman, rare for many of the towns and cities in México or anywhere, for that matter. He had never had any children—sadly his wife could not have them—and so he was essentially alone. His solitary life got him down at times, but there always seemed to be a case or a child that needed extra attention, and he was eager to help whenever he could.

The other police officers and patrolmen respected Lieutenant Mendez and his expertise in crime fighting. He was often consulted on cases not his own, and his superior allowed him a great deal of margin with his decisions and methods in dealing with a case.

On top of the stack of papers on his desk was a picture of a lovely young woman identified as Gloria Bernabe. Under the first picture was a photo of a corpse found in the city dump. The corpse had been identified as Bernabe.

What a shame, Lieutenant Mendez thought. She hadn't been on any missing persons lists. She had no arrest sheet and was not a *puta* (prostitute). Her death was a homicide; the coroner said her throat had been slashed and she had bled to death.

He had discovered the identity of her latest boy-friend, Lenny Elmwood, a *gringo*, living on the outskirts of Chihuahua. This afternoon he'd ride out to his place and question him.

He'd already visited the stage show, *Arriba Abajo* (Bottoms Up), where Gloria had worked as a dancer. Her boss hadn't seen her in two weeks. He'd had to replace her in one day and he wasn't happy that she had never notified him that she was quitting.

Mendez picked up his sunglasses and headed for his Chevrolet Caprice in the parking lot. He took the thoroughfare to the north of Chihuahua, turned off on Camino Antigua to the west, until he saw the sign along the road, Vista de Pajaro. He turned into the long dirt trail to the Elmwood place. At the end of the driveway he could see the screen door hanging on just one hinge. He went up the porch steps and knocked before trying the doorknob. The door was unlocked and he entered the house. It smelled like a tenement and he could tell that it was recently abandoned. There was no rust ring in the toilet and the electricity was still on. Objects were scattered everywhere, pillows had been ripped open, drawers pulled out and thrown on the rug. In the kitchen he saw the same thing, canned foods thrown on the floor of the pantry, chairs overturned. The bedrooms were an equal disaster. The house had been searched and ransacked. Fortunately he found no bodies. Out back the chickens were free ranging and scratching in the dirt. In the chicken coop he found a dozen eggs in various nests. He stashed as many as his pockets would hold and scattered some chicken feed on the ground. There were no vehicles in the yard front or back. Several deep tire tracks behind the chicken coop were apparent, as if a couple of vehicles had torn away from the premises in a big hurry.

Mendez took out a small notebook from his pocket. He wrote down what he had discovered at Lenny Elmwood's residence. He locked the front door from the inside and then left by the back door. It appeared that Elmwood was missing also. He'd alert the dump manager to the possibility that another body might be showing up soon. He shook his head sadly at the turn of events.

≳≲

*L*enny, Lola, Sherry and Clint were seated around the table. Lola was the first to speak.

"I'm so sorry about Gloria, Lenny. I feel like I caused her death." She put her hand on Lenny's arm.

"I'm sorry too, Lola, and thanks, but it's not your fault. Whoever killed her probably thought it was you. He's on my list now. He's going to get what's coming to him when I find him." Lenny's fists were doubled up on the table.

"I understand that, Lenny, and I would like to give pay-backs too, but these people from Las Vegas, they are killers, not men who let their guard down long enough to give them a pay-back." She took a deep breath. "I saw them kill my boyfriend, Tony, in Las Vegas. They slashed his throat. I saw both of the men. One of them is dead thanks to a good friend, a bar owner who owned a gun and wasn't afraid to use it. She killed him just before he was going to shoot me. I remember vaguely what the other man looked like; he had reddish hair, and a flushed complexion. I prayed I would never meet up with him again."

Clint lit a joint and passed it to Sherry. "Do you think the Vegas Mob would send the same man down here to…kill you?" He asked.

Lola nodded. "I think so. He knows what I look like. Of course they have dozens of pictures of me. All my publicity photos for the theatre where I danced are their property."

"Thankfully you look different out of make-up," Lenny said.

"We could just pick up stakes and all four of us go to Puerto Vallarta or Acapulco on an extended vacation," Lola suggested. "Sherry and I have enough money to last quite a while."

"No, we are not running," Lenny said. "We need to fight back; this has to end for Lola and it's going to end in Chihuahua with me — us getting the bad guys."

"But Lenny," Sherry said, "How can the four of us fight against professional killers?"

"I'm not sure yet, but I know we'll find a way." He took the joint from Clint and they exchanged looks.

"Me and Lenny can be a couple of pretty tough *hombres* when the need arises," Clint responded.

"So we're all agreed," Lenny said, looking around the table, "we do not run away. We stand and fight."

Lola looked at Sherry. Sherry nodded. "I'm with you. I want Lola to be safe again."

Lenny looked at Lola his eyebrows raised. "Lola, you in with the rest of us?"

She smiled at the bravado of her friends and perhaps their foolishness. "I'm in," she said.

⊰⊱

*L*ola and Sherry were coming back from the rest-room at the Chihuahua Enchilada Restaurante when they saw the children at the front window. Sherry could make out the little girl with the blue dress.

"See Lola, they're back," Sherry said pointing to the children.

Standing in back of the five children, Lola noticed the woman to whom she and Sherry had given the $200 in the cardboard hovel at the city dump.

"Yes, I see, and their mother is with them."

One of the little girls waved to Lenny and Clint as Lola and Sherry stepped outside. The mother approached them.

"*Las señoritas, estoy agradecida por el dinero*," (I am thankful for the money) she said shyly.

"*No problema*," Lola answered, smiling.

"*Esto es para ustedes*," (This is for both of you) the woman said, thrusting a package into Lola's hand.

"*Gracias, señora, gracias*." Lola said. "*Señora, como se llama?*" (What is your name?) Lola asked.

"Maria Valdez."

"Maria, we want to help you with your children. How can we help?" Lola put her hand on Sherry's arm and said she would tell her later what was being said.

"You have helped very much", Maria said. "I can never repay you."

"No payment is expected."

"*Por favor*," Maria said, motioning at the gift.

Lola opened the sack and took out two packages of brand-new socks, still wrapped in their cellophane. She held them up to Sherry. "*Gracias, Señora* Valdez. They will keep our feet warm." Lola handed the package to Sherry.

"*Sí, gracias, señora,*" Sherry echoed.

"Won't you come into the *restaurante* with the children and join us for lunch?" Lola invited.

Maria shook her head. "No, no, it would not be permitted."

Lola nodded. "Oh yes, it will. I will speak to the owner. There will be no problem. Please, come, and bring the children."

Maria looked almost overwhelmed, her eyes began to tear up, and she looked up at Lola as if she had just flown down from the sky in Quetzalcoatl's arms (an ancient winged sky-serpent and legendary ruler of the Toltec people in México).

Lola stood with the door open. "*Entre, Señora Valdez y sus niños.*" (Come in, Mrs. Valdez and children.)

Meanwhile, Lenny and Clint were watching the entire event. Maria called to her children and they ran under Lola's arm holding the door and right to the table where Lenny and Clint were busy adding enough chairs for everyone to have a seat.

The *restaurante* owner, by now being well acquainted with Lola and Sherry's determination to feed the children, came out of the kitchen. Lola assured him that the children and Maria were invited in by her and that their lunch would be paid.

"Are you sure, *señorita*? This is a lot of mouths to feed."

Lenny stepped in. "No problem, *señor*. We will pay."

Lenny held the chair for Maria, and she looked up at him as if she could hardly believe what was happening. Her children became very quiet and looked on with large, round eyes. When everyone was seated, Lola asked Maria if there was any food the children didn't like. Maria shook her head

"Should we order combo plates for everyone?" Lola asked looking from Lenny to Clint to Sherry.

"Good idea," Clint said.

The lunches were ordered and Lola asked Maria to introduce her five children.

Maria started with the small girl with the blue dress. Speaking in Spanish, she introduced each of her five children. "Ines, she has five years, Rosa has six years, Chado has seven years, Federico has eight years, Luisa is the oldest at nine." She pointed to each one as she said their names and ages.

Ines was very small and delicate with large dark eyes and brows that swept her forehead like wings. She was also quite shy and rarely spoke in the company of strangers. Rosa was more animated; her lovely eyes and turned-up nose were always moving. Chado was quiet like his sister, Ines. He nestled in the shadow of his brother, Federico. Federico was large for his age, and quite vocal. He and Luisa were the spokespersons for themselves and their siblings. Louisa was a picture of beauty, looking the most like their mother. She was outgoing and full of energy like her sister Rosa. All the children had lovely dark hair and copper-colored skin.

Sherry was sitting next to Ines, and she put her hand on her head and stroked her long glossy hair. She smiled up at Sherry.

"Oh boy," Clint said to Lenny. "I can see this is going to be a vocation for the girls."

Lenny smiled and agreed. "They need something to take their minds off this other thing."

The food came on three large trays carried by two young men from the kitchen. They were amused and laughed among themselves at the *barrio* children eating in the *restaurante*.

Lola interrupted them and spoke in Spanish. "Understand, we want to feed them, that's all. We are not going to harm them in any way. And you will not laugh at them."

The boys sobered and finished serving the plates than hurried back to the kitchen.

Maria explained to Lola it was difficult for them to believe she and her children were being fed out of kindness.

"Yes I know," Lola said, "Don't give it another thought."

The five children dug into their plates and ate like they hadn't had food in days. Maria ate very slowly and tried to slow the children down but finally stopped trying. She smiled and shrugged at the four *gringos* and quietly returned to her plate.

"What exactly are we going to do about them, long

term?" Sherry asked.

"I'm not sure," Lola answered. "I'm wondering what kind of education we could arrange for them. Do you think they could go to school?" Lola directed her question to Lenny and Clint.

Clint and Lenny both laughed. "I don't think you could get any school to take in *barrio* kids. And they would have to start in the first grade, with children much younger than they are," Clint said.

Lola had a faraway look in her eyes. "I would like them to have some schooling. What would private lessons cost here in Chihuahua?" She directed her question to both of the men.

Lenny shook his head. "I haven't a clue, but we could ask *Profesor* Gilberto at the university."

Lola felt the *profesor* was a kind and wise man. Her eyes sparkled. "Yes, that's a great idea, Lenny."

The children finished eating everything on their plates. There wasn't even a grain of rice left. Maria was trying to keep them quiet until she finished.

"We have to have dessert," Lola said with a smile. "*Helado, sí?*" she asked the children.

"*Sí, sí,*" they all chorused.

She ordered ice cream for everyone, insisting that Maria have a dish, too. Maria was very thin; Lola suspected she sacrificed her own portions of food to feed her children.

When the ice cream arrived, the waiters were very polite and served the children and Maria without laughing.

"*Gracias,*" Lola said, thanking the waiters to show she noticed their good behavior.

When everyone was finished and Lenny and Clint paid the bill, Maria took her leave, thanking and bowing to Lola and Sherry in deference.

Lola lifted the woman's chin and said, "Walk tall, Maria. You are a proud mother. Sherry and I will help you. May we come to your home soon?"

"*Sí, señorita.* You are always welcome." The children had departed the *restaurante*, waving at the four *gringos*. Maria followed, but looked back twice at the four Americans as if she wanted to be sure she hadn't dreamed the entire meal.

Lenny and Clint left a nice tip for the waiters and waitress that had served them. The four of them climbed into the VW, full and happy.

When they returned to Los Campos, Sherry and Lola each gave Lenny and Clint some of their money to make up for the amount they spent feeding the children.

"You don't have to repay me," Lenny said.

"Yes, we do," Lola insisted. "This is Sherry's and my project. You and Clint are wonderful to help but we want to pay for the expenses."

Lenny shrugged. "Okay. How long your money lasts depends on how much and how long you two intend to help Maria and her children. Have you thought of that?"

Lola and Sherry exchanged looks. "Yes we have, but we haven't come to any definite decisions yet about how long or how much," Lola said.

"I can help with the money," he said.

Clint gave a big sigh. "Yeah, me too. I have more money than I can spend."

"Thanks, both of you," Lola said.

Sherry kissed Lenny on the cheek and Clint on the lips to show her thanks.

≋

Jack Marchetti disembarked from Southwest Airlines in El Paso, Texas. He had already arranged for a late model rental car to drive into México. At the border he said he was going on vacation for a week.

Once in the city of Juarez he called Raul DeSilva, the contact Guido had given him, to pick up a .22 handgun with a silencer. With the gun tucked under the seat he set out for his destination.

It would be a five hour drive to Chihuahua, according to his calculations. If the roads were halfway good he'd make it by evening. Then he'd find a cheap motel and tomorrow he'd meet with Juan Bolero. Bolero had Lola in his clutches but had let her slip away. He might just kill the guy for being so stupid.

Jack's partner, Martin Fellino, had met his death in Mohave Valley, Arizona last year at the hands of a zealous bar owner who thought Martin was holding up the place. Jack could never understand how a woman could get the draw on Martin. He was supposed to be taking out Lola Raines-Morales. Instead, he became a gunshot death statistic.

Finally his boss in Vegas got a lead on Lola; she was spotted in Chihuahua, México. But the last time he made this trip, he'd killed the wrong girl. She was a real looker, a dead-ringer for the Morales woman. Based on her photos he thought he had the right person, especially since Bolero had fingered her.

A secret fear was growing in his belly like a tumor. He was afraid, at times, he was losing his skills. Little things began to go wrong. He'd forget to do some small detail, or... kill the wrong target. He couldn't fuck up this time or the boss would take it out on him. This matter had gone on too long. All because the Morales girl *might* have seen him and Martin kill Tony Ricco, the casino manager in Vegas.

That entire episode in Vegas happened over a year ago. He and Martin were told to 'hit' Tony Ricco, a casino manager, because he was skimming. Apparently they had left a loose end—Tony's girl, Lola—alive. She wasn't at Tony's plush home in the Las Vegas Country Club Estates, but he *had* found her nightgown on the floor. Based on that trivial piece of evidence, Martin had been told to find the girl and kill her. She had gone to Arizona and hidden out in a small town. Martin found her and, just as he was about to hit his target, the owner of the bar where Lola worked shot him, thinking he was robbing the bar.

Jack headed south in his rented gray Camaro. Five hours later he came to the outskirts of Chihuahua. He found a small hotel in the downtown district and rented a room for a week, paying with cash. Actually, he was planning to take care of his business and be out of here tomorrow or the next day.

He picked up the room phone and called Bolero.

"*Hola.*" Bolero's deep voice came over the line.

"*Hola.* This is Jack from Vegas. We need to talk about the Morales girl."

"She visited her old boyfriend at his house. I can give you his address."

"Okay."

"She was staying at Vista de Pajaro on Camino Antigua. I had a man guarding the house. The owner of the house, Lenny Elmwood, came back and tied my man up and took clothes from the house. She's gone. Don't know where they went."

Jack cursed under his breath. "I'll take a ride out there tomorrow morning. Then I'll need to see you again."

"Okay. Come to the warehouse around noon."

"I'll be there," Jack said and hung up. What an asshole! He'd let the Morales woman and her boyfriend slip through his fingers. Jack would just have to find her himself. It might take a bit longer than he thought at first, but he'd paid for a week at the cheap hotel.

He reached up and touched his cheek where a long nail scratch was healing. His last hit had dug her talons into his face before he cut her throat.

He went across the street to the Chihuahua Enchilada Restaurante. A quick meal, early to bed, and he'd be up before dawn and out to the Elmwood place.

≋

*F*or a little diversion the four of them decided to take a train ride through the Copper Canyon. Lenny explained it was known as Barranca del Cobre by the locals, it was home to the Tarahumara Indians, famous for their love of long-distance running. The Tarahumara resided in remote villages throughout the canyons. There was no electricity in the villages; they had lived this way for thousands of years.

Copper Canyon was part of the greater Sierra Madre range of mountains. The rugged and isolated terrain of mountain peaks was populated with pine and oak, while the canyon floor was the home of sub-tropical forests. Legend said that the black bear and puma were still seen in the canyons, but the deer and wild turkey were rare, having been over-hunted.

They drove to Creel, at 7600 feet above sea level. The landscape was high desert, with scrub brush, large cactus, both saguaro and ocotillo, resplendent with their large orange blossoms, as well as prickly pear cactus here and there along the dirt road. Creel was the starting point through the canyon. They had the option to ride on the train through the entire canyon, which would take the best part of a day, or get off at any of the many village stops and return on another train to Creel.

Lenny and Lola took a seat in the second car, and Clint and Sherry sat right behind them.

Lola was enchanted by the many waterfalls that could be seen during their ride. Massive cliffs reflecting the sun gave Copper Canyon its name.

Lenny sat holding Lola's hand as they gazed at the hues of sierra and copper splashes across the face of the cliffs. It was relaxing not to think about being in danger and all the other problems that she was facing. She enjoyed the warmth of Lenny snuggled close to her.

She pondered why she'd left Lenny years ago. The thought of getting close to someone after the pain of living with her parents must have terrified her. Being twenty years old and inexperienced could have something to do with it, too. Many times she had regretted breaking up with him. But she had gone on with her life, began a career dancing in Las Vegas, and all the excitement of the Big City made her forget her first love.

Now that she was with him again, there was something unfinished between them. If she could get beyond the killer stalking her, she might be able to concentrate on something else in her life. At the very thought, however, of a permanent commitment with Lenny, Lola felt a chill slide down her back in spite of the hot weather. It hadn't worked between them before. What made her think it would work now?

When the train went through the multiple tunnels carved out of the mountain side, Lola looked behind and noticed Clint kissing Sherry. She deserved a partner that cared about her as Ronnie had cared. If it hadn't been for the train wreck in Arizona in which Ronnie was killed, Sherry would probably be living with or even married to Ronnie. Funny how different events affect each other and how strange life can be. Lola knew definitely that she wouldn't still be with Billy Jim, even if he hadn't grieved over Ronnie's death to the point of pushing her away and trying to strangle her. His domineering behavior would have gotten old even if he hadn't gotten physical with her. Lola felt that usually things worked out the way they were supposed to, an attitude that made it easier to accept change and consequence.

At the third village, they disembarked and got on a train going back to Creel. Creel itself had only two dirt roads and was a primitive village. They found a simple *cantina* with half a dozen tourists eating. A table in the back was available. They ordered tortillas, beans and *cervezas*.

Lola sat on a small stool. "That was wonderful. I totally forgot about our troubles while we rode around that gorgeous canyon."

"Me too," Sherry said with a big smile.

Their food arrived and they all began eating with gusto.

"We aren't out of the woods," Lenny said between bites. "We can't stay at Diego's place forever. Eventually I want to move back to my ranch."

Clint put down his *cerveza*. "I've been thinking. We have to bait this guy from Vegas. Somehow get him on our territory and have a showdown with him."

Lola's eyes widened. "You mean a shoot-out?"

Clint nodded. "That's exactly what I mean. You'll never be safe as long as he's alive." He looked at Sherry. "Neither will Sherry."

"Yeah, I was thinking along those lines, too," Lenny said, glancing at Lola. "This killer, the only language he knows is killing. We'll just beat him at his own game. There are two of us, only one of him."

"What if he comes with a backup? Another guy… uh…killer," Lola interjected.

"We'll deal with it," Lenny said.

"There is also Juan to consider, and his two henchmen," Lola said.

"I suspect the hit man will not want any help from Bolero. He already screwed up his assignment to keep you locked up," Clint suggested.

"There are four of us with guns," Sherry added. She did a little pantomime drawing imaginary guns at her sides. Everyone looked at her and began laughing.

After the release of some pent-up tensions, Lola felt considerably better. She was shocked at first that the two of them would even consider killing the man that was after her. But of course that was what the killer was told to do to her! In a strange, revengeful way, it made sense. Maybe she should send a message to the bosses in Vegas telling them she would never divulge anything she'd seen. But then they would know for sure she had seen the murder. They would send someone else, and on and on. It made her head hurt to think about it. She just wanted to be safe again.

"We'll wait for the right opportunity when we think he's seen us; then we'll lead him back to my uncle's place," Clint suggested.

"I'm not sure that's a good idea," Lola responded.

"I don't want him to know where we are. Then he can take us unawares."

"Let's think about this some more, before we do anything," Lenny said. The four of them agreed.

"Something I've been thinking about." Lola looked at the three faces turned toward her. "I may have to change my identity and my appearance for good. That may be the only way I can escape ever being found by 'them' again."

Clint nodded. "That can be accomplished fairly easily here in México. In fact, I know a guy who makes false I.D. papers."

"That sounds like a good idea," Lenny said. "We should work on that right away."

"What would you change your name to, Lola?" Sherry asked.

"How about Lily?" Lola suggested. "That's close enough to Lola."

"What about a last name?" Clint asked.

"I was thinking Elmwood would be a nice last name for you," Lenny said with a grin.

Lola looked at Lenny and saw the twinkle in his eyes. "Is that a proposal?" The words flew out of her mouth without her thinking.

"If you'd like to be my wife, it sure is." Lenny put his arm around Lola and kissed her on the cheek. "Or if not, we could pretend for the outside world. You could use my name."

"Wow, I can't believe it," Sherry hooted. "You just got proposed to, Lola."

"Hey, I think that's a damn fine idea and solution to your identity problem," Clint said grinning.

Lola sat in stunned amazement. Marriage was something she and Lenny had never discussed, even in their early days. She knew she wasn't ready for marriage, but an arrangement for as long as they both agreed on could save her life. She could be and look like someone else. The more she thought about it, the more she liked the plan.

"Okay, we need to get you some new identity papers and change your looks. The killer knows what you look like," he said.

Clint and Lenny split the bill and they left the *cantina*, climbed into Lola's VW and headed back to the cottage outside Los Campos.

PART II
Friends and Enemies

$\mathcal{L}$enny, Lola, Clint and Sherry spent a day moving Maria and her children to a room in a boarding house on the edge of the *barrio*. The rent was very reasonable and Lola and Sherry shared the cost of the six months rent in advance; the landlady was elated that she had such a good paying boarder. She allowed Maria and her five children to have a hot plate in the large, sunny room, as well as a small refrigerator that Lenny and Clint had brought in, and a slop bucket for toilet use. There was a bathroom with a shower at the end of the hall but eight other people used it also. Sherry and Lola had purchased bedding for the double bed and four cots had been moved into the room. Maria was ecstatic at the size and cleanliness of her new surroundings and promised the girls she would keep it in that condition.

There was a small card table and two over-stuffed chairs. A lovely window seat under a large bay window pleased the children, and they jockeyed to see who would get to sleep there first.

Maria still had a large portion of the $200 that Sherry and Lola had originally given her. She was proving to be very frugal. Lola assured her she would not let them go hungry. After Maria and her children had arranged their new purchases, the girls took her to the *mercado* to buy some food, while Lenny and Clint took the kids to a local place for *helados*.

"I think Sherry and Lola are getting as much pleasure out of this as Maria and her children," Clint said to Lenny at the ice cream parlor.

Lenny nodded. "Yup, that's why they thought this project up. They have this money they didn't expect, and I think they wanted to do something good with it. They certainly chose a great outlet, helping the Valdez family."

Ines and Rosa finished their cones first. "*Gracias, señores*," they said to Clint and Lenny.

Clint laughed. "*De nada, niños*. You know, Lenny, I'm getting as much fun out of this as Sherry and Lola."

"Me too," Lenny said.

Clint looked at Lenny closely. "I got the impression at first that you weren't overjoyed at the arrival of Lola and Sherry. Now you seem to have warmed up to Lola. Inviting her to share your name is a big step."

Lenny nodded. "I wasn't particularly happy about her showing up, at first. I didn't want to revisit all the pain and shit I went through when we broke up. But this time around it seems to be different. I decided to be thankful for small gifts and favors. And yeah, I offered my name in any way she wants to use it. I think I know her well enough to know she won't marry me. But with Elmwood for a last name, no one will connect her with her old identity." He smiled at Clint.

"What would you do if she took you up on your proposal?"

"I guess I'd take her in a flying millisecond."

"You love her?"

Lenny nodded. "Always have."

"I figured that, watching you two together."

What about you and Sherry?"

"I'm falling fast and deep," Clint said with a big grin.

The waitress brought the check and the guys split it. When the children were finished, Lenny and Clint took them back to their new room. Maria and the girls were back from the *mercado* and were putting food away in the cupboards and refrigerator.

Maria kept chattering to the children in staccato Spanish about the wonderful food items they had bought. The oldest girl, Luisa, began helping her mother store the goods.

When the work was finished, the four *gringos* bid their new friends goodbye.

"We will come by every few days to make sure all is well, *comprende?*" Lola said to Maria. "Don't feel you have to stay here if you have things to do. If we don't find you at home we will leave a note under the door."

Maria pulled Lola and then Sherry to her in a hug. "*Gracias* to you both from the bottom of my heart," she whispered in both their ears. Ines started to leave with Lola; apparently she had made a big impression on the littlest girl.

Maria pulled her back, "*No, niña*. She will be back."

They all laughed at Ines' attachment to Lola. Sherry and Lola hugged her and Lola told her in Spanish they would be back in a couple of days.

When they climbed into the VW, Clint said—not meaning to be unkind—only practical, "You girls have bitten off a large bite. I hope you realize that they will probably have to go back to the dump if and when you no longer have money to support them."

Lola quipped, "We realize that. That's why we're going to find Maria a job."

Lenny and Clint laughed. "You two are full of surprises," Lenny said.

≳≲

Jack spun the chair behind the desk one time around and Juan's body fell to the floor. He pushed the chair away from the desk and began opening drawers. In the second one he found two photos, one of the woman he'd already killed, and one of Lola Raines-Morales. Juan had told Jack that Lola looked different from her publicity photos. Then Jack had cut his throat.

Putting the photos in an inside pocket of his jacket, he headed for the door, stepping over the bodies of Juan's two henchmen. It was a shame these men were so badly trained. They hadn't even pulled out their guns before Jack shot them both in the head.

Jack Marchetti climbed into his Chevy rental car and headed out to Vista de Pajaro.

⧓

Lola looked in the mirror. She hardly recognized the woman staring back. The reflection showed she now had a very short hair-do, a French cut, Sherry said, and it was a shiny auburn hue. Her bangs had been combed to one side across her forehead and the sides of her hair swept onto her cheeks like a French adagio dancer she had once seen in a movie. The back was very short; shingled, Sherry called it.

Sherry had plucked her brows into a new line and added a touch of eyeliner to emphasis her already large eyes.

Lenny came into the kitchen and whistled. "Wow! Who do we have here? Is she a French movie actress? Or maybe a Mexican film star," he joked.

"She certainly looks different," Sherry agreed. "More glamorous."

"I'm not supposed to attract attention. Maybe we should forget the eyeliner," Lola commented.

"I think it looks great," Lenny said. "When we go out you can wear sunglasses. I have an old pair of horn-rimmed glasses with just glass in them, too. Why don't you try them on for a more conservative look?" He went to find them in his room. When he returned Lola tried them on.

Her reflection still presented a nice-looking woman, perhaps adding a few years.

"I like that look, Lola. How about you?" Lenny asked.

"It's okay, if it's a departure from the way I used to look."

Sherry cocked her head and looked at Lola. "Yes, I think the glasses complete the picture. Let's go with that for your public image."

"Say, where'd you learn to cut hair like that, Sherry?" Lenny asked.

"I went to cosmetology school in Phoenix just out of high school. But I decided it was too boring, so I never really worked as a hair stylist."

"You certainly made Lola look good," he said.

"We'll put Clint to the test when he returns. See if he recognizes her," Sherry suggested.

When Clint returned an hour later from town, he walked into the cottage and was startled to see a strange woman in the kitchen with Sherry. Lola had tied a small pillow around her waist and hips and put on one of Lenny's sweaters. She looked to have gained 20 pounds.

"Hi." He stopped and looked at Lola. "Who's this?" He stared at her for several minutes. Finally Sherry burst out laughing and so did Lola. "Damn, is that you Lola? You sure look different. I think you've hit on a concealing combo — change of hair and adding the glasses. But how did you gain weight so fast?"

Lola lifted the sweater to show Clint the pillow tied around her middle.

"Perfect. If you fooled me for a minute, you will fool others."

"That photo that Juan has of me," Lola explained.

"That was a promo picture when I was in complete stage make-up. That's not what I look like normally."

"I think we need to stay out of Chihuahua for a while. There's no way anyone would connect us with Los Campos," Clint said.

"I agree. But we do have to make one trip into town to get Lola some new I.D. papers," Lenny reminded the others. "We'll pay a visit to Clint's contact tomorrow and see if we can get them done soon."

Clint took a joint from his pocket. "How about a little smoke? We all need to relax a bit. We've been too uptight lately."

"Sounds like a good plan," Lenny said as Clint handed him the joint.

≋≋

*J*ack turned at the sign that read Vista de Pajaro. The dirt road slowed him down a bit as he avoided the potholes. In the distance he saw a Spanish-style adobe house with a long veranda built across the front. He parked in the drive, got out and went up the front porch steps. The screen door was partially open, hanging on one hinge, but the front door was locked. It was fairly simple to spring the lock instantly when he inserted his wire-thin lock pick. He opened the squeaky door and went inside.

Stepping into the living room he saw evidence that the house had been searched. He checked all of the rooms, saw the broken furniture and scattered clothing, and deduced that no one was living here. In the corners of the bedrooms there were piles of dust and feathers. As near as he could tell from Juan's jumbled English, Lola was visiting the boyfriend of Gloria Bernabe, the woman he had killed. That's why she showed up at the warehouse in the company of her friend. This was the house of Gloria's boyfriend, Lenny... He couldn't remember the last name. Besides their close resemblance the boyfriend was another connection between Gloria and Lola.

He didn't give a shit what the connection was; he just wanted this job over. One trip had been wasted already and now he needed to find Lola and end it. He had been paid after killing Gloria, but he wasn't getting paid to take care of Lola. This trip was on his nickel.

In the master bedroom there was a photo of Gloria and a guy, probably the man who lived here. Slipping it out of the frame, he took out the photo and added it to the other two in his pocket.

There was nothing else to learn in this place. In retrospect he realized that Juan would have made this easier for him, but of course it was too late now. Juan had tried to get some more money out of him, and that had really pissed him off. He had cut Juan's throat as he sat in his chair.

⋙

*L*enny, Clint and Sherry had eaten grilled chicken (Lola had eaten leftover's) and corn on the cob on the back porch, and were sitting around the campfire in the back yard smoking a joint. When the fire burned down, Clint and Sherry said goodnight and walked hand in hand into the cottage. Sherry and Lola had been sleeping in twin beds in the only bedroom; Clint had been sleeping on the porch on a cot and Lenny on the couch.

Lenny slid over next to Lola and put his arm around her. "I think Clint and Sherry are going to use the bedroom tonight. Okay?"

Lola looked up surprised. "Did Clint say something to you?"

Lenny nodded.

"Sure, that's okay. I can sleep on the porch." Lola stared into the fire. Wow, she'd missed the road signs. She hadn't realized Sherry was ready to sleep with Clint. But of course, why shouldn't she? Lola felt Sherry should get on with her life romantically and not live in the past. There would always be memories of Ronnie, but they won't keep her warm at night. Maybe she should start thinking about her future, too. It wasn't good to continue putting Lenny off, or he might give up. She was sure she didn't want him to do that. So far, they had traded a few kisses and hugs, nothing more. He had asked her with his eyes several times to lay down with him, and she had turned away.

"Are you about ready, too?" Lenny asked.

"Yes," Lola said realizing the double meaning.

Lenny poured a bucket of water over the coals, and they went to the screened back porch, arm in arm. There was a small cot with a sheet and blanket folded on the end. She turned to Lenny and put her arms around his shoulders and kissed him. His lips met hers and he back-walked her over to the cot. This time she sat down and pulled him with her. They lay down, their legs entwined. Lola unbuttoned her blouse and unhooked her bra. Lenny kissed her collar bones, her shoulders, and then the nipples of each breast.

"It's been a long time, but your body is as familiar to me as my own," he murmured.

He slipped off her jeans and panties and quickly shed his jeans and shirt. "You know I've always loved you Lola. I've never forgotten you."

She smiled and kissed his mouth quiet. His mouth was hard but urgent; his hands exploring all the nooks of her body. He bit her on her neck; little love bites, remembering that had always aroused her. She reciprocated by kissing his stomach, working her way further down, which was something Lenny had always desired.

When he entered her she shook in remembered ecstasy. He started slow and easy and she moved in rhythm beneath him. Soon his strokes became faster and deeper and finally he gave one long deep thrust and groaned. In a few minutes he slipped out and slid down to her thighs and began to pleasure her. Lola squirmed and moved her pelvis to a rhythm of her own. Suddenly she lifted her hips high and gave a long, low moan.

Lenny slid up to her mouth and kissed her tenderly. He embraced her for a long time, lying on top, supporting his weight with his arms. Finally he moved to her side and pulled her tightly next to him.

"This is where I want to be, Lola." He said, softly.

She sighed with satisfaction. "Me, too."

※※

Clint shut the bedroom door and took Sherry in his arms. They kissed passionately, and Sherry suddenly pulled free and slipped her tee-shirt over her head. He saw her gorgeous breasts that needed no bra. He picked her up and laid her on the bed. Thrusting off his clothes quickly he began undressing her.

When he entered her, for one second the memory of Ronnie's love-making flashed across her mind. Then she pushed it away and enjoyed this new experience and pleasure that Clint was giving her.

Sherry immersed herself in the sensations of Clint's skillful lovemaking. She returned his kisses and stroked his muscular body. After he came, she moved on top and quickly came to a climax. She slipped down beside him and they cuddled spoon-fashion.

"Sherry…" Clint murmured.

"Hmmm…?"

"I want you to stay with me. Don't go away. I'll protect you."

Sherry lifted her head and looked over his shoulder. "What do you mean, go away?"

"I mean I don't want you to go if Lola and Lenny decide to leave this area."

She laid her head back down. "Okay. I hear you."

"Will you stay with me?"

Without thinking about the decision, Sherry said, "Yes."

Clint gave a long sigh and immediately fell into a deep sleep.

God, she'd just committed to a long-term relationship! What was she doing? She'd suddenly decided without talking to Lola that she would not continue traveling with her if Lola decided to leave. That was a major decision for her — a girl who had a hard time making decisions in the past. Maybe she was gaining a measure of maturity. That thought pleased her. She still felt immense sadness at the loss of Ronnie, but he would want her to get on with her life. And Lola had encouraged her to do that, too. She knew instinctively that Lola would not be unhappy when she told her she was committing to Clint.

≳≲

Lieutenant Mendez entered the old warehouse and followed his Sergeant into one of the rooms along the dark hallway. He stepped over two bodies near the door and walked over to the desk, rolling the body on the floor over with his foot. The fat man had a deep cut across his throat. Entirely too many bodies were turning up with slashed throats.

"Who discovered the bodies?" he asked Sergeant Marin.

"Apparently two kids who were playing hide and seek. They told their parents and one of the fathers called headquarters." The Sergeant held a handkerchief over his nose.

"How long do you think they have been here?" Mendez asked.

"The coroner hasn't been here yet, but I'd guess three or four days."

Mendez walked to the two bodies near the door. He examined them and saw the gunshot wounds in their heads. "Someone is pretty proficient with a knife and gun. Get me I.D.'s as soon as you can." The two policemen walked out of the rundown warehouse, got in their car and headed back to the police station.

Counting Gloria Bernabe and these three males, that brought the body count to four in two weeks. This was an unusual amount when they seemed non-gang or drug-related. And then there was the missing Lenny Elmwood. He wanted to question him about his girl-friend, Gloria. Mendez had put out a Police Bulletin Alert but so far no one had spotted him.

⋙⋘

*P*rofesor Gilberto was seated at his desk when Lola and Lenny entered his office. Looking up he said, "Come in, come in. How nice of you to drop by. To what do I owe this pleasure?" The *profesor* looked at

Lola carefully. "I approve your change of appearance and I understand the necessity for it."

"Thank you, sir," Lola said.

They took seats across from the *profesor*. "Sir, Lola has an interesting proposition she wants to run by you." Lenny turned to Lola.

"Sherry and I have adopted a family in the *barrio*. Maria Valdez has five children and we recently moved her into a room in a boarding house. We paid six months' rent for her. She had been living in a cardboard shack at the city dump. We would like to find a tutor or tutors to teach each of her five children how to read and write. Depending on the interest and aptitude of her children, some of them might want to continue their education. Sherry and I will pay for the tutors. We thought maybe you know a suitable tutor among your many students." Lola sat back in her chair as she finished her request.

Profesor Gilberto laid down his pen, and took off his glasses. "My goodness, that is certainly a wonderful thing to do. What possessed you girls to want to do this?"

Lola warmed to her subject. "We have some money that a good friend left us in his will. He did a wonderful thing for us. We want to pass the good fortune on to others. Maria and her children were barely surviving at the city dump like so many families do. She is trying hard to care for her children."

"I see," the *profesor* said. "You realize when you leave and her six months' rent is up, she may have to go back to the dump to live?"

"Yes, we do. That's why it's imperative that we find Maria a job. Something she can earn money at, so that she can be self-sustaining."

"My, you girls do think big," he said, laughing.

"The girls took Maria out and bought her sheets and blankets for the beds in the room, plenty of food, six chairs and a table for them to eat on; they have really taken this family into their hearts," Lenny added.

Profesor Gilberto stared out the window across the campus. "I believe I can find a couple of students who would love to earn extra money to tutor the children. What are their ages?"

"Luisa is the oldest at nine, Federico is eight, Chado is seven, Rosa is six, and the youngest, Ines, is five."

"We should definitely give lessons to all of them, but wait a year for Ines," the *profesor* suggested.

Lola nodded. "I would consider it a favor if you would decide how much to pay the tutors. Sherry and I want to give them a fair wage."

Profesor Gilberto laughed. "You are certainly an exceptional young woman, as is your friend Sherry." He turned to Lenny. "You'd better keep this lady around."

"I'm going to do my best," Lenny said.

"All right, I'll get started right away. I think we can find someone to tutor the two older children, and another tutor to teach the six and seven year old. Does that meet with your approval?"

Lola nodded. "Thank you so much, *Profesor*. Sherry and I really appreciate your help in this."

"Think nothing of it. Now to the problem of finding

Maria work. I think I can get the department to hire her. She can be added to the housekeeping staff at the archeology building, and she can clean my office, too. We've just recently let one of our cleaning persons go. How does that sound?"

Lola felt her heart expand with gratitude. "That sounds wonderful! Thank you again; you've made things easy for us."

"My dear, I wish there were more people in the world with your compassion and sensitivity." He turned to Lenny. "Thank you, young man, for introducing me to Lola and Sherry." The *profesor* stood up. "Call me in two days and I will have two students lined up." He shook hands with Lenny and Lola and waved goodbye as they left his office.

Profesor Gilberto sat back down in his comfortable chair. He was always in awe when human beings behaved like Lola and Sherry. Giving the gift of food and an education to these children was an extraordinary offering. Without the American women's help, they would live out their lives on the garbage dump of Chihuahua. Indeed the women were extraordinary individuals. Lenny better hang onto Lola. From what the *profesor* picked up intuitively and from what Lenny said, he figured Lenny had every intention of doing that. Lola was a darn sight better match for him than that dancer, Gloria.

⋛⋚

*J*ack walked the streets of the downtown *barrio*. Coming up was a video store. He entered, went to the counter and asked for Roy.

"*Quien usted?*" the clerk asked.

"Jack from Vegas."

The clerk walked in back behind a curtain. He returned with a short man with a glossy mustache and little sharp eyes.

"*Que pasa?*" he said to Jack. He motioned him to follow him in back through the curtain. Roy sat down at a desk and Jack remained standing.

Jack had met Roy on his first trip down when he mistakenly killed Gloria thinking she was Lola. Roy was one of the two contacts the Vegas boss gave him in Chihuahua. Juan was the other.

Jack pulled out the photo of Lenny and Gloria. "I need to find this man, *pronto*," Jack said in Spanish.

"I thought you wrapped up your business a couple of weeks ago?"

Jack hated to admit he made a mistake. "Uh… hit the wrong target. I'm looking for this woman." He pulled out the photo of Lola.

Roy studied it carefully. "A real looker; resembles the other one."

"Yeah," Jack said. "Know her?"

The man looked vaguely familiar but Roy couldn't place him. He shook his head. "You ask Juan? He may know where this man is."

"I asked him. He told me where he lived, but he's moved on."

"I'll ask around," Roy said. He held out his hand. Jack laid a $100 U.S. bill in it.

"Where you stayin'?" Roy asked.

"I'll be back," Jack said, ignoring Roy's question as he went out through the video store.

※※

*G*uido Carscione pressed the button on his desk for his secretary. An attractive blonde woman entered his office, hair swept back in a chignon, short skirt, and long slim legs enhanced by high heels. Guido insisted that his female employees wear high heels. He thought women looked frumpy in low-heeled shoes.

"Cindy, has Jack Marchetti called?"

Cindy shook her head. "No sir, nothing so far."

"How long has he been gone on assignment this time?"

She flipped her notepad back a few pages. "He left on the third of the month. He was supposed to report back in five days. It's been seven."

Guido snapped his fingers in frustration. "Damn. I hope he hasn't blown it again." Nasty business, taking out the wrong woman, he thought, unwilling to share everything with Cindy.

The secretary waited quietly.

"Get him on the phone."

Cindy left the office and closed the door. In a few

minutes Guido's phone rang. "Yeah," he spoke gruffly into the receiver.

He heard Jack's voice on the other end.

"What the hell's going on?" Guido complained. "Does it take you a week to do an assignment?" He was silent for a moment, then, "Jack, get this done. No screwups. Understand? You got three more days." Guido hung up. He picked up his unlit Cuban cigar, stuck it between his teeth and clenched down on it in frustration.

Cindy knocked and reentered Guido's office. "Would you like anything else, sir?"

"Get me a scotch and water, Cindy," he ordered.

The secretary went to the bar and poured the drink, adding ice from the small, built-in refrigerator. Her eyes scanned the Jackson Pollack painting behind Guido's desk to make sure it was hanging straight. Her boss had a thing about paintings that hung in a crooked manner on his walls. Glancing around the room at the de Kooning, the Andrew Wyeth, and the Andy Warhol pieces, she was satisfied that all was well with Guido's art collection.

She set the drink in front of him on his bamboo desk.

"Will that be all, sir?"

Guido nodded and took a slurp from his scotch. Cindy turned on her beautiful legs and left the office.

Christ, it was a shame that Martin got blown away by some hick bar-owner in Arizona last year, Guido grumbled to himself. He was a good man, always carried out his assignments; that is, until the last one. Lola Raines-Morales proved to be a difficult hit. He'd give

Jack as few more days, then he'd send someone else to take out Jack along with Lola. Guido had no patience with incompetent hit men.

≥≤

*L*enny, Lola, Sherry and Clint were crammed into Betsy, headed for downtown Chihuahua in the *barrio* where they could get some false I.D. papers for Lola.

Lenny parked in front of a video store. They crawled out of the little Beetle and entered the store. There were no other customers in the place. Clint went to the counter while the other three held back.

"Roy, *por favor?*" he asked the man behind the counter.

"Who wants to know?" the clerk asked in Spanish.

"Tell him he did some work for me a couple of years ago, some papers." Clint answered.

The clerk disappeared behind the curtain and Roy returned with him. Roy looked Clint up and down.

"What you want?" Roy said in English.

"Could we talk business?" Clint asked, taking a wad of U.S. currency from his pocket.

Roy motioned him to follow and they went behind the curtain.

Presently Clint returned and gestured for Lenny, Lola and Sherry to follow him. They all went to the back of the shop.

Lola noticed the place smelled like dirty socks and stale cigarette smoke. Papers and videos were piled in stacks everywhere. Strips of wallpaper hung down on one wall, as if someone had started to take it off and stopped in the middle of the chore. The man whom Clint wanted to do business with sat down behind an old scarred desk; newspapers, books and videos were scattered on top.

Clint gently pushed Lola in front. She had tied a pillow around her waist and she wore a long Mexican shift with bright flowers. Her hair was a shiny auburn. She had on the horn-rimmed glasses Lenny had given her and she looked nothing like the girl who had arrived a few weeks ago on Lenny's doorstep.

Lenny spoke up. "We want a driver's license and a passport in the name of Lily Elmwood."

"It will cost you…" Roy said.

"*Cuanto?*" Lenny asked.

"Three bills," Roy answered.

Lenny took two $100 dollar bills out of his pocket and handed them over to Roy. "You'll get the rest when we get the papers."

Roy folded them quickly into his pocket. He pointed for Lola to sit in the chair in front of the camera.

Lola sat down and Roy snapped six pictures of her. "I'll need some information. What you want filled in on date of birth, place, and occupation?" he said.

Lola took a pen from the table and a pad of paper. She wrote, 12/16/55 — Chihuahua, México for place of birth, and waitress for occupation. She handed the paper to Roy.

"Come back in three days, I'll have them ready. Where you staying?"

Clint spoke up. "We're staying at a friend's up north. We'll be back in three days."

The four of them left the video shop and crawled back into the VW Beetle.

"Wow, that was easy," Lola said.

≋≋

As soon as the front door closed, Roy made a beeline for the front counter. "You take my truck and follow their car." He pointed out the front window at the VW. "Come back here afterwards." Roy handed his truck keys to Ramon, the clerk. "Don't let them see you following them, and be careful with my truck."

After Ramon had left out the back and jumped into Roy's truck preparing to follow the VW, Roy remembered that Jack from Vegas was looking for a guy named Elmwood. But neither of the women looked like the woman Jack was hunting. He'd have to be careful revealing that one of the women was getting a false passport and driver's license. His reputation was based on the guarantee that he kept his mouth shut. Yet he wanted to turn Jack onto this foursome because of the name Elmwood.

≋≋

Halfway back to Los Campos, Lenny knew they were being followed. The same truck had pulled behind them at the video store and was still behind them two cars back.

"We got a problem here," he said to Clint in the back. "We're being followed. How we gonna lose him?"

Lola started to turn her head around, but Lenny

stopped her. "Don't," he said, grabbing her wrist. Clint slid down in the back seat and peeked out the bottom of the back window. He saw the green truck two cars back, but couldn't see the person driving.

"That jack-ass Roy must have put a tail on us," Clint grunted under his breath.

"I'll try and lose them before we turn down the dirt road to town." Lenny slowed down and the two cars passed him on the highway. The green truck fell back so as not to get too close to the VW.

"We're coming up to the grain storage building with the little *cantina*. I'll stop there and we'll go in for a drink." Lenny pulled off the highway and parked in front. The green truck went on by, slowly, and kept going down the highway.

They piled out, went in and bought colas and sat down on the porch. In five minutes, the green truck passed by again going the other way.

"What should we do?" Lola asked.

"I think we should just sit here for another hour and discuss what to do. Maybe he will give up and head back to Chihuahua," Lenny said optimistically.

After the colas were finished, Clint went in and brought out four cervezas. They sat in the shade of the porch. The green truck never passed by again.

I think we need to bypass Los Campos and spend the night in the next town. We can't afford to lead him to my uncle's place," Clint said.

Lenny thought that was a good idea. "What is the next town?"

"Santa Isabel," Clint said. "It's only another ten miles. But it's large enough we can find a couple of rooms in the low-rent part of town."

Once in Santa Isabel they were able to find two rooms next to each other in a run-down boardinghouse. The sheets didn't look too clean, Lola thought, but they weren't going to undress. The four of them ate a light dinner at a local *cantina* and retired early. The plan was to get up around midnight and head back to Los Campos, hopefully without a tail.

≋≋

When Ramon returned late that night, he stopped at the video store where he knew Roy would be waiting.

"Where they go?" Roy demanded.

Ramon told Roy he followed them to the town of Santa Isabel to a boarding house.

Santa Isabel was south of Chihuahua, not north as Clint had said, Roy thought. Well, if Jack came in or called he could turn him on to their destination. Of course, that didn't mean they would stay put. There were a lot of tiny villages in that area. They could be holed up in any one of them.

Two days later, Lenny, Lola, Clint and Sherry headed for Chihuahua in the VW to visit Maria and the children and tell her the good news that *Profesor* Gilberto had found Maria a job and that he had arranged tutors for the four older ones.

Lola was in her usual disguise and Sherry wore a straw hat and a long Mexican dress with lots of beautiful embroidery on the bodice. Lenny felt they were safe enough with Lola's changed appearance.

The boarding house where Maria and the children were living was busy as they entered. Several youngsters were playing on the steps, and two old ladies were rocking on the porch smoking their cigarettes. The four of them walked down the hall to Maria's large room and knocked.

"*Quien es?*" Maria called from behind the door.

"Sherry and Lola," Lola answered.

Maria opened the door with a wide smile on her face. She welcomed them in with open arms for the girls. She patted Lenny and Clint on their backs.

"*Entren, por favor,*" she said to the four of them. "*La Señorita Lola se cambio.*" (Lola has changed).

"*Sí Maria, es necesario,*" Lola explained.

The four of them looked around. Maria had hung curtains at the windows, and a tablecloth was spread across the table. Dishes were stacked neatly at the small kitchen sink area. There was a double bed in one corner with a brightly colored bedspread that Lola and Sherry had picked up, and four cots stacked in the other corner of the room. Rosa and Luisa were sitting near the large window that gave a view of the back yard. The sun warmed the cushions that Ines was curled up on, and the bougainvillea spilled into the room through the open window. Lola took in a deep breath of the fragrant scent. Flowers and bushes were planted around the edges of the yard. A small vegetable garden took up one corner of the area. A table and several chairs could be seen just outside the back door.

The three girls came up and hugged Sherry and Lola, one at a time. When greetings and hugs were given all around, Lola took Maria's hand and motioned her to sit at the table.

"Maria, we have some good news," Lola explained in Spanish. "*Profesor* Gilberto, a friend of Lenny's is going to have two of his students tutor Luisa, Federico, Chado and Rosa so they can learn to read and write. Ines will get her schooling next year."

Maria was surprised. "*Que?*" she asked.

"Yes, Maria, your children will learn to read books and write their names. Isn't that wonderful? And Sherry and I are taking care of the cost. We want to do this for you and your children."

Maria began to cry and covered her face with her hands.

"It's okay, Maria. We're happy for you. Does this please you?" Lola asked putting her arm around Maria's shoulders.

"*Sí, sí, señorita, estoy es muy contenta,*" (Yes, I am very happy) she said, wiping her eyes.

"And we have one more piece of good news. You are to start a new job tomorrow morning, working at the university, cleaning the archaeology building. You will be part of the housekeeping staff. You can begin as early as you want. Two other women will be working with you. You have all day to do the cleaning. Also you will clean *Profesor* Gilberto's office. We will take you in the morning to meet the *profesor* and then you will begin. You can ride the bus to the university after tomorrow."

Maria stared wide eyed as if she could hardly believe her ears. "*Dios mio*," she said softly.

"Luisa can stay with the children while you are working," Sherry added. "You will only have to work three days a week. The *profesor* will go over your work schedule when you meet him in the morning."

Luisa and Rosa were clapping their hands in joy as they knew what this meant for their family. There would be steady money coming in.

"Sherry and I will continue to give you money also to supplement your income," Lola said.

"*Gracias, señoritas*, I can never repay you for these favors," Maria said.

"There is no need to repay. We are happy to help you," Sherry said, all smiles.

"How about we all go to lunch and celebrate?" Lenny offered. "Where are the boys?"

"They are out on the streets making money," Maria said proudly. "But forgive me, please eat with us." Maria jumped up and went to the small refrigerator. "*Por favor*, sit down and eat with us." She took out homemade tamales and put them in a pan to heat.

Lola translated to Lenny, Sherry and Clint what Maria had said. The girls looked at Lenny and Clint and the guys nodded their approval.

"I've wanted to try out Maria's culinary skills," Lenny said as he and Clint took their shoes off and sat on the old couch that Maria had found somewhere and moved into the apartment.

While the tamales were heating, the boys, Federico and Chado, came bursting into the small apartment. They greeted the four new friends and wanted to know what was for lunch. Maria chattered at a rapid rate to her children, giving them instructions to set the table. When everything was ready, she served Lola two tamales first, telling her they were corn only — *sin carne* (without meat).

"How sweet, Maria, that you remembered. *Gracias*," Lola replied.

The guests were seated at the table with Maria while the children sat on the chairs and couch to eat.

Maria bowed her head, as did her children, and offered a prayer of gratitude to the four Americans for their kindness. The five youngsters dug into their lunch and ate as only growing children can.

After lunch, while Maria and Luisa were cleaning up, Sherry looked at a picture book with Rosa, and Lola held Ines on her lap, telling her a story. Federico and Chado were digesting the news that their mother was telling them about their learning to read and write and about Maria's new job. Clint and Lenny were laid back on the sofa digesting their delicious lunch.

⧓

*L*ieutenant Mendez read the report that the lab had submitted to him. The dead man in the warehouse was identified as Juan Bolero, a small-time gangster and owner of a night club. The other two dead men were his henchmen. No drugs or contraband was found in the warehouse, but in Bolero's desk, behind the false bottom, several thousand American dollars was found. Mendez confiscated the money, turning it over to the Department. His Police Chief congratulated him saying, "good work."

None of Mendez's informants had spotted Lenny Elmwood. He was still a missing person although no one had reported him as being missing. In Mendez's considerable experience as a police officer, most people who went missing were never reported. Not in México. There were just too many people who disappeared mysteriously. Sometimes they were found, usually dead, but often they were never heard from again.

He decided to pay a visit to Roy, one of his informants he hadn't contacted lately. Perhaps he'd heard something in the *barrio* regarding Elmwood.

Mendez drove to the *barrio*, parked around the corner, locked his car and entered the video shop.

"I'm here to see Roy," he said to Ramon, the man behind the counter.

"Yes sir," Ramon said, as he hurried to the back.

Roy pulled the curtain back and said, "In here."

Mendez walked through the curtain and Roy offered him a chair beside his desk.

"Que de nuevo?" (What's new?) Roy asked.

"How are things in the video business?" the lieutenant asked, ignoring Roy's question.

"Not bad. People maybe don't have much *dinero* but they find enough to rent videos."

"I know you don't get your income from just rentals, Roy. What have you heard on the street about an American named Lenny Elmwood?" Mendez lit a cigarette and leaned back in the chair.

Roy was startled but covered his surprise expertly. "Ah...I heard some things."

"What things?"

"My information is from the U.S. Maybe a little chumming would help me remember."

Mendez sat up straight. "Listen, you little creep. Don't try that shit with me. I know you get your monthly stipend from the force. That's to keep us informed. Now what do you know about Elmwood?"

Roy held up his palms in submission. "Okay, okay. I hear there's a hit man from Vegas looking for him."

Mendez looked surprised. "Is he in town now?"

Roy nodded.

"Has the hit man found Elmwood or is Elmwood in hiding?"

Roy hesitated. He didn't want to give away too much. He still had to give something to Jack. "I think Elmwood is in hiding. I heard he is protecting an American woman, Lola Morales, who is the real target of the Vegas people."

Mendez contemplated this information. "Why are the Vegas people interested in this Lola Morales?"

Roy shook his head. "*No sé*, Lieutenant," (I don't know).

Mendez stood up. "You let me know if you hear anything regarding this hit man or Elmwood. *Comprende?*"

Roy nodded. Mendez turned and went through the curtain to the front of the shop.

"*Hasta la vista*," Ramon said as Mendez slammed the door.

Mendez walked across the street to the Chihuahua Enchilada Restaurante to have some lunch and consider the information he'd just received. Elmwood had been Gloria Bernabe's boyfriend. She had turned up dead at the city dump. Mendez had visited Elmwood's ranch outside of town and found it abandoned. Elmwood knew he was being hunted.

≶≶

Sherry and Lola were on their way to Maria's to take the children out to lunch. Maria had started her new job and was at the university working. After lunch the girls would swing by the university and pick up Maria.

"Is there enough room in the back for all of them?" Sherry asked.

"I think we will have to drop the boys off here and then go pick up Maria." Lola said as she maneuvered into a parking spot in front of Maria's boarding house.

Sherry got out of the VW quickly and hurried into the house, returning within a few minutes with all five children.

It was a short drive to the Chihuahua Enchilada where all seven of them piled out of the VW and entered the *restaurante*. Lola led them to a table and the proprietor waved from the doorway to the kitchen. After the waitress had taken their order, Lola looked over the five children.

"What have you been doing this morning while your mother is at work?" she asked Luisa.

"Rosa and I cleaned the room and put on a pot of beans for dinner," Luisa answered.

"I looked at my new picture book you gave me," Ines said proudly.

"Wonderful, Ines," Lola said. "I'm glad you like the book."

The boys, Chado and Federico sat politely until Sherry spoke to them. "What did you two do this morning?" she asked.

The boys spoke a little English they picked up on the street. "We work in garden for lady who owns house," Federico said.

Chado nodded. A strip of black hair hung over one eye. "I help digging," he said with a grin.

"We need to take the boys to the barber. They need haircuts," Lola noted.

Sherry brushed the hair away from Chado's eye. "We can do that next time we come into town."

When the food was set before the children, they started eating, heads down as if they hadn't eaten for days.

"You'd think these children never have enough food," Lola commented, watching them.

Luisa stopped eating. "We have plenty to eat now that we have our large room and the stove and refrigerator.

Mama feeds us good, thanks to you." Suddenly embarrassed, Luisa bent her head and began eating again.

"We are happy to help," Sherry said, holding back the emotion that threatened to spill out in front of the children. She looked at Lola and blinked her eyes to thwart the tears.

Lola patted Sherry's arm. "Eat up, everyone. We have to pick up your mother soon."

The children topped off their meal with a bowl of *helado* and every dish was as clean as if it had been hand-washed.

Lola and Sherry paid the bill and they all left the *restaurante*, climbing back into the VW.

No one noticed the man standing on the corner behind a signpost watching them.

After dropping the two boys off at the boarding house, Lola drove to the university where Maria was waiting for them in front of the archaeology building. She climbed in back with the three girls, holding Ines on her lap.

"How was your second day at work?" Lola asked.

Maria smiled. "Very good, *señorita*. I clean *Profesor* Gilberto's office but he say, no touch anything." She shook her head. "Very hard to clean that way."

Lola and Sherry laughed. "So, the *profesor* is a neat freak," Sherry said in English. "I knew he must have one quirk. He couldn't be as perfect as he first appears."

Lola drove back to the boarding house, parked, and they all climbed out and went into Maria's studio apartment. The boys were not there.

"Did you leave the boys here?" Maria asked.

"Yes, we dropped them off before we picked you up. We assumed they came in the house."

"They probably went out. They are very independent and are used to being on the streets. They will be home soon." Maria said.

Lola and Sherry stayed for another hour but the boys did not come back. "Do you think we should go out and look for them, Maria?" Lola asked, somewhat worried.

"No, no, they will be home eventually, *señoritas*. *Gracias* for taking them all out to lunch. It was very kind."

"Our pleasure," Sherry said. "The tutoring starts next week. We will come by to pick them up the first few days until they get used to going."

"*Gracias señoritas*, I am very appreciative of what you do for them," Maria said.

"We know and you are very welcome." Lola took a card from her purse and handed it to Maria. "This is *Profesor* Gilberto's phone number. In case of emergency, be sure to call him. He will get in touch with us. Can you read the numbers?"

Maria took the card and looked at the phone number. "*Sí, señorita.*" She placed it in a drawer in the chest. "*Gracias, señorita.*"

"*Hasta la vista*, Maria, we will see you on Monday," Lola said as she and Sherry hugged Maria and the girls and left.

⋙⋚

*J*ack had followed the two women that Roy had told him about, one of them getting a false I.D. in the name of Elmwood. He had said they were driving a VW with Arizona plates. He saw them go into the Chihuahua Enchilada Restaurante and waited for them to come out. Neither of them looked anything like the photo he took from Juan's office, but they were the women with Elmwood. Killing them would cover his ass in case one of them was Lola Morales. He could whack them now but he didn't like hitting his targets in broad daylight on a street. The kill-zone should be of his choosing; better for him to get away.

Jumping into his car he followed them and hung behind at a safe distance, pulling up in front of the boarding house after the two women left. He entered the building and walked down the hall until he saw an open door. Federico and Chado were sitting at the table. Jack recognized them as the boys getting into Lola's VW at the *restaurante.*

He spoke hurriedly in broken Spanish; "Boys, your mother is hurt. She asked me to come and get you."

Federico looked stunned. "But *señor*, my friends have gone to pick up *mi Madre* just now," he said.

"I am telling you she wants you there now," Jack said, impatiently.

The boys jumped up from the table without further questions and followed Jack out to his car. When they were in the back seat they asked him a lot of questions in Spanish, but Jack couldn't understand them.

"Be patient. I am taking you to your mother," he assured them.

He drove into the vacant lot of the old warehouse where he had killed Juan.

Bewildered, Federico said, "*Señor, por favor*, is my *Madre* here?"

"Yes," Jack insisted. "She's had an accident."

Chado and Federico followed Jack obediently into the crumbling building, and he led them into the very room where Lola had been detained.

Seeing the *gringo* remove a coil of rope from beneath the cot, Federico made a move for the door, but Jack grabbed him by the hair and tied his hands and feet. Federico struggled but Jack slapped him on the back of the head and the boy felt dizzy. Chado was paralyzed. He couldn't move and he wasn't leaving his brother here alone. When Jack was finished tying up Federico, he tied Chado's hands and feet and put a long strip of cloth around both boys' mouths. Then he threw them on the cot.

"No one comes around this deserted warehouse, boys," Jack said in broken Spanish, "so don't think your new friends will rescue you."

Federico and Chado were struggling on the cot to try and kick off the ropes around their ankles.

"I'm not going to hurt you; I just want to hold you until I can get your friend *Señorita* Lola here. Once I get her, I'll let both of you go." Better to let them think they will get their freedom. That was a basic rule in his training as a hit man. "Do you know where *Señorita* Lola is staying?"

Federico shook his head. Chado did nothing.

"I mean it, if I find her I will let you two go, but if not, well, too bad." Jack made a motion horizontally across his neck, making it very clear what he would do to them.

"I'm going to see your mother. She will tell me where the *gringa* woman is to save her boys."

The boys stopped wiggling and looked at each other. Federico watched Jack leave the room and heard him lock the door. He looked at his little brother. Tears were rolling down Chado's cheeks into the rag around his mouth. If only they hadn't climbed into the car of the man who said their mother needed them immediately. Federico knew he should not have fallen for that trick; he was much too street-smart. But he had.

He rolled over to Chado's side and laid one leg across his brother's leg. Looking into his eyes, he winked and nodded his head. He was trying to let him know they'd get out of this fix. He didn't want to get *Señorita* Lola in trouble with this bad hombre. He hadn't told him where she was because he truly didn't know. Even if he had known he wouldn't have told.

≷≶

*J*ack drove to Maria's boarding house. He parked down the street, walked to the back of the house and entered through a rear door. He knocked and waited. Maria opened the door just a short distance.

"*Quien es?*" she asked.

"I have news of your boys," Jack said in Spanish.

Maria opened the door wide. "They all right?" she asked anxiously.

He looked around the room and saw the other children were not in the room. "They are fine, *señora*. However, I must tell you that they will only be returned if you tell me where I can find *Señorita* Lola." Jack spoke matter-of-factly but he was intent on getting an answer.

Maria understood English better than she could speak it, but she shook her head. "*No comprendo, señor*. Why can I not have them back now?"

Jack tried to be patient. "Because I am holding them hostage until I have the *señorita* in my custody. Do you understand me now?"

Maria looked at him in disbelief.

"Now tell me where I can find her."

Maria shook her head again. "*Yo no sé*," (I don't know) she said.

"You'd better find her as soon as you can. Put out the word. Do you know anyone else who knows her?"

Maria wisely shook her head a third time. "*No, señor*." Tears began to form in her eyes.

Jack sighed. "When will she be back to see you?"

"*Yo no sé*," Maria said.

"When she returns, you tell her she must call this number immediately if you ever want to see your boys again, do you understand?" Jack laid a card on the table.

"*Sí, señor*," Maria replied, choking back more tears.

Jack let himself out of the apartment and went down the hall to the back door.

Maria cried until her shoulders shook. After a few minutes, she dried her eyes on her apron, took a piece of paper from the shelf in the cupboard and went down the hallway to her landlady's apartment. Maria knocked.

Señora Martinez opened the door. "*Sí, Señora Valdez. Que paso?*"

"*Señora* Martinez, may I use your phone? It is an emergency or I wouldn't ask. My boys are missing and I need to call someone who will know what to do."

"*Sí, señora.* Come in. The phone is over there." She pointed to the corner of the room.

Maria dialed the number on the piece of paper Lola had given her.

"*Hola,*" *Profesor* Gilberto's voice came over the phone.

"*Profesor,* this is Maria. I need your help; my boys are gone and a man came and said he was holding them hostage. He said he would only give them back if he got *Señorita* Lola instead." Maria began to cry again.

"Don't cry, Maria. I'll send a policeman to you immediately. Stay in your room and he will come very soon, I promise."

"Thank you, *Profesor.*" Maria hung up, wiping her wet face.

Señora Martinez couldn't help but hear the conversation. "*Señora* Valdez, who has taken your boys and for what purpose?"

"I don't know," Maria replied.

"Where are your girls?" was *Señora* Martinez' next question.

"Outside, looking for Federico and Chado."

Señora Martinez went into the hallway with Maria and was walking her back to her room, when the three girls burst in the front door.

Luisa saw he mother crying again. "We didn't find them," she said.

"Yes, I know," Maria answered.

"*Señora*, you come down to my apartment if you need anything. I'll be home all day and night." The landlady squeezed Maria's arm.

"Thank you, *señora*, you are very kind."

"*De nada*," *Señora* Martinez called as she returned to her apartment.

The three girls and their mother went inside their room and shut the door.

Maria explained as well as she was able what had happened to their brothers. She told the girls that she had called *Profesor* Gilberto and he would call a friend, a policeman, to come and help.

Profesor Gilberto called an old friend at police headquarters, Lieutenant Gus Mendez. The policeman was not in but he left an urgent message to call him immediately. He explained to Sergeant Marin who took the message what had transpired with Maria's children and the sergeant promised the *profesor* he would make sure Mendez received it the minute he was in touch with him.

⚔⚔

A few minutes later, Mendez's radio came alive. "Mendez, Mendez, check in." The lieutenant heard his Sergeant calling over his radio.

He picked up the receiver and said, "Yes, Sergeant, what's up?"

"Call came in from *Profesor* Gilberto at the university. Says his new employee, a cleaning lady by the name of Maria Valdez, reported her two boys missing. And the kidnapper paid her a visit." Marin explained all that was said to the *profesor*.

"What's the address of *Señora* Valdez?" Méndez asked.

"*2700 Verde Calle. Numero tres.*"

Mendez hung up and called *Profesor* Gilberto. He heard the same information; however, the *profesor* said to bring Maria and the girls to his house for safekeeping. Mendez drove the five minutes to Maria's boarding house. He parked in front and went up the front steps to the entrance. A young girl was sitting in a chair on the porch. He asked where he could find the apartment of Maria Valdez. She motioned for him to follow her and she led him down a hallway to *numero tres*. He followed her inside where he found two other girls sitting in chairs at a table with a woman, obviously the mother. She was crying with her hands covering her face.

"Mama," Luisa said, "this man is asking for you."

Mendez immediately identified himself as a policeman. "I'm Lieutenant Mendez."

Maria looked up and dried her eyes on the back of her hand. "My two boys are gone. They didn't return last night. *Señorita* Lola told me to call *Profesor* Gilberto if an emergency arose."

Maria took a deep breath. "A *gringo* came here this morning and said he had my boys and he would return them if I told him where to find *Señorita* Lola. I told him I didn't know where she lived. He said I'd better get in touch with her or someone who knew where she was if I ever wanted to see my boys again." A fresh gush of tears came and Maria sobbed into her hands. When she caught her breath she said, "I called *Profesor* Gilberto because I didn't know what else to do."

Luisa was patting her mother's back and Rosa and Ines had climbed down from the table and put their arms around their mother's shoulders.

Lieutenant Mendez also put his hand on Maria's shoulder. "Don't worry, *Señora* Valdez, I will find your boys and return them to you. Meanwhile I want you and your girls to be safe, so I would like to take you to *Profesor* Gilberto's home to stay for a few days, until this mess is cleared up. He has graciously offered for you and the girls to stay with him. Will that be all right with you?"

Maria wiped away the tears again. "Oh *señor*, we don't want to be a burden to *Profesor* Gilberto. He has been so kind, giving me a job."

"No problem, I assure you. Please pack a few clothes for you and the girls and I'll drive you there immediately."

Luisa and her mother went to the chest and started pulling items from the drawers and putting them into a cloth bag. When they finished, Maria took a card from the cupboard.

"The *gringo* gave me this number to give to *Señorita Lola* next time she visited," Maria said.

Mendez took the card and recognized the phone number as the hotel across the street from the Chihuahua Enchilada Restaurante. "Thank you, *Señora* Valdez," Mendez said as he put the card in his pocket.

Who was this *Señorita* Lola that Maria kept referring to? And why did the kidnapper want to know her whereabouts? He wondered if she could be Lola Raines Morales that the Vegas Mob sent a hit man to find. He would ask the *profesor* who she was and why she was of interest to the kidnapper of Maria's boys. Why had he promised this mother to find and return her boys? That was a risky promise and one he might not be able to keep. He desperately wanted to help this woman, and he hated anyone who preyed on children.

The lieutenant took a close look for the first time at the mother, Maria Valdez. She was quite attractive, with long shiny black hair pinned in a bun at the nape of her neck. Her large dark eyes were brimming with tears. The loose, faded dress she wore had seen many washings.

He took the bags from the girls as they all left the room. Maria locked the door behind them. They walked to the unmarked police car and got in the back. The lieutenant drove them to *Profesor* Gilberto's home located in a nice neighborhood. Maria noticed the houses were farther apart, they had drapes in their front windows and the yards were tidy and well kept.

The car stopped at a particularly nice home. Everyone got out of the car and went to the front door. The *profesor* had seen them drive up and greeted them.

"*Buenas tardes, Maria.* Welcome children, please come in." He opened the door wide, extended his arms and invited them inside. "*Sientense, por favor.*" (Please sit down).

Ines stayed at her mother's side, but Rosa and Luisa walked into the hallway and immediately took seats in the living room. Maria followed and she and Ines sat on the couch. Lieutenant Mendez took off his hat and followed the *profesor* into the living room.

"Please have a seat, Lieutenant."

When everyone was seated, the *profesor* asked if any of the girls or Maria wanted food or drink. Maria answered, "*Nada, gracias,*" for all of them.

"I have plenty of room and I would consider it a favor for you to stay until we get the boys back," the *profesor* said.

"*Gracias, Profesor,*" Maria said.

"Tell me the names and ages of the boys, *Señora* Valdez," the lieutenant asked.

"Federico is eight and Chado is seven," Maria answered, "but Federico is large for his age. He could pass for age ten or eleven."

"Did the man who visited you give you his name?"

Maria shook her head.

"That's all right, try not to worry. I'll be in touch soon."

"*Gracias, Señor Méndez,*" Maria said.

He took the *profesor* aside and asked him if he knew who *Señorita* Lola was and where she was staying?

"She and her friend Sherry Brown are an amazing couple of American girls. They have taken Maria and her children under their wing and have helped her tremendously." *Profesor* Gilberto told the lieutenant the entire story. "I believe Lenny Elmwood said they were staying at his friend Clint's uncle's cabin. But I don't know where that is," the *profesor* said.

The *profesor* told Mendez how he knew Lenny. The lieutenant began to see the connections. *Señorita* Lola *was* the woman that Roy said was being hunted by the Vegas people. The man who kidnapped Maria's boys was obviously the hit man sent to kill *Señorita* Lola.

"If Lola Morales or Lenny Elmwood gets in touch with you, please find out where they are and call me immediately," the lieutenant told the *profesor*.

"Of course, I will."

The lieutenant took his leave of Gilberto's home and climbed wearily back into his car. It was clear that Lenny Elmwood and his two friends knew they were being hunted and were in hiding. Now, where would a *gringo* unfamiliar with the city of Chihuahua stash two little boys where he thought no one would stumble onto them? Mendez figured the hit man killed Juan Bolero, the night club proprietor and owner of an unused and crumbling warehouse near the *barrio*. The warehouse was just a few minutes from Maria's room. He stepped on the gas and headed for the abandoned building.

><

*F*ederico tried to comfort Chado as best he could with his hands tied behind his back. He had managed to slip the handkerchief from around his mouth by rubbing it on the dirty mattress.

"Chado, don't cry. We will get out, I promise. Just be patient."

Federico pulled off Chado's mouth rag with his foot. Chado's tears had soaked the cloth and mucus made it hard for him to breathe through his nose.

"*Hermanó* (brother), I'm afraid. He will kill us," Chado gasped.

"No Chado, we will get away. I promise." Federico fervently prayed that someone would find them before the man looking for *Señorita* Lola came back. If he didn't find her the man might kill them.

On the way to the warehouse the lieutenant called Sergeant Marin to meet him there. Marin left word with the dispatcher where they were going and to stand by in case they needed reinforcements.

The two undercover police cars stopped a block away and Marin and Mendez walked to the warehouse.

"If the hit man is in here, we may have a battle on our hands," Mendez said.

Marin nodded. "How do you know the boys are

being held there?"

"This is the only isolated spot the hit man is familiar with here in Chihuahua. It's a good guess, but I want us to be prepared in case we can't take him alone."

"No problem, boss," the Sergeant said, "We can take him."

"Be careful of the boys," the lieutenant warned. "We don't want them hit by our fire."

Mendez entered the back door of the place, Marin right on his tail. They drew their Smith and Wesson .38 specials and proceeded very quietly down a dark hallway. About half way down they heard a child's voice speaking and another child whimpering.

"Try not to worry, Chado, I'll think of something to get us out of here."

The two police officers found the room the voice was coming from. Mendez motioned Marin to continue down the hall to the main room and see if it was occupied. Mendez waited quietly in front of the door. He heard more quiet murmuring inside, but he couldn't make out the words.

Marin went through the archway and checked the main room, returning to the hallway shaking his head.

The lieutenant turned the knob carefully. It was locked. He put his shoulder to it and forced it a couple of times with no luck, then he stood back and shot the lock off the door. When he opened the door he saw the two boys lying on the cot, eyes wide, one of them crying. Their hands and feet were tied.

"We are the police. Don't be frightened. Where is

the man who did this?" Mendez asked.

"He's left, but he said he'd be back," Federico said.

Sergeant Marin untied the hands and feet of the smallest boy. "What's your name?"

The child was shaking and did not answer.

"He's my brother Chado, and I'm Federico," the larger boy said.

"Are either of you hurt? Did he hurt you?" Sergeant Marin asked.

"No," answered Federico, "but he said if he didn't find *Señorita* Lola he would…." The boy showed them the motion across his throat that Jack had made.

"Are you the sons of *Señora* Valdez?" Mendez asked, as he finished untying the rope on Federico's feet. He knew the answer but he had to ask.

"Yes," Federico answered.

"We will return you to her immediately. I want to get you both out of here before he comes back. Come with us, quickly."

The small boy, Chado, could hardly walk so Mendez picked him up and slung him over his shoulder. Marin took Federico's arm and they moved quickly down the hallway and out the back door, walking the block to the cars. The two boys were put in the back seat of Sergeant Marin's vehicle. Mendez climbed in the passenger side, leaving his car in the alley.

"Could we have some water?" Federico said.

The lieutenant pulled a thermos from beneath the seat and handed it to the back. Both the boys took long drinks. "Can we drink it all?" Federico asked.

Mendez nodded and exchanged looks with Marin. "We are taking you to your mother and your sisters. They are staying at *Profesor* Gilberto's home, temporarily."

The boys were silent, having emptied the contents of the thermos.

"Can you tell me anything about the man who held you hostage?" Mendez asked, looking in the rear view mirror.

"He had red hair, red skin and green eyes, I remember that." Federico said. "And he said he would let us go if he found *Señorita* Lola. We didn't know where she lived, but even if we did we wouldn't have told him," Federico said, bravely.

"I'd say you two were pretty courageous boys." Sergeant Marin said.

"We should never have got in his car; he said our mother was sick and needed us immediately," Federico said.

"It's understandable why you did. Did he say anything else about where he was going when he left?" Mendez asked.

"No, *señor*," Federico said.

"His car is a gray Chevy Camaro," Chado spoke for the first time.

Mendez glanced in the back seat. "You say he was driving a gray Chevy Camaro? How do you know that, Chado?"

"I know cars," was all Chado said.

"Chado's hobby is cars," Federico explained. "He knows all the makes and models."

"Thank you very much for that piece of information. That will help us a lot," Mendez said with a smile.

"How are you boys feeling? Are you hungry? Want to stop for some food?"

Both boys shook their heads. "We want to see our mother, please," Federico said.

"Okay, you got it. We're almost there."

The two boys jumped out of the car as soon as Marin pulled up in front of *Profesor* Gilberto's house. They ran to the porch, then, as if remembering their manners, waited for Mendez and Marin to catch up.

At the lieutenant's knock, the door was immediately opened by *Profesor* Gilberto.

"Please, come in," he greeted the two policemen and Maria's two sons.

Federico and Chado bolted through the door and ran into their mother's waiting arms.

Amid tears and hugs the boys embraced their mother and sisters, everyone wiping their eyes. Maria patted the couch on each side of her for the boys to sit.

Lieutenant Mendez introduced Sergeant Marin to the *profesor* and Maria.

"Where did you find my boys, Lieutenant?" Maria asked.

"I found them in an abandoned warehouse. I knew the kidnapper had been there before, so I figured that might be the only vacant place he knew."

"Did you catch the bad man?" she asked Mendez.

"Not yet," Sergeant Marin answered. "But we are

on his trail."

Maria turned back to her boys, kissing them on the tops of their heads.

"Now Maria" the *profesor* said, "I want you to treat my house as your own. There are two rooms in back. The boys can have one room and you and the girls the other one. I've set up extra beds so everyone has a place to sleep. You may cook for your family; I believe I have enough food in the cupboards and refrigerator. I'm not much of a cook, I'm sorry to say. You can stay home from work for a few days; I think the crew at the university can get along without you. Your children need you right now, and I want to remind you, the children's tutoring begins tomorrow. Please bring the two girls to my office about 3 p.m. It's a short walk from here. I'll bring them home when they are finished."

"*Gracias, Profesor*, I will do that." She turned to the two policemen. "*Gracias* from the bottom of my heart for saving my son's lives."

Mendez looked a little embarrassed, but both he and Sergeant Marin nodded and smiled. "No problem, at all, *Señora*," Mendez said.

"Can we speak to you privately, *Profesor?*" Mendez asked.

"Of course. Maria, I am taking the policemen into my study. Why don't you prepare some salsa and chips for our guests and the children? We'll be out in a minute."

The *profesor* led the men to his study and closed the door. "Have a seat, gentlemen."

Mendez and Marin sat in the two chairs in front of *Profesor* Gilberto's desk where he was seated.

"I want you to be very careful at work; don't mention to any of your co-workers what has occurred or that Maria is staying here. We don't want this man showing up. *Comprende?*" Mendez said.

"Of course, Lieutenant. I won't say a word. Maria and her children are safe here, I believe."

"I'll have a car drive by at night periodically," Mendez said, "and if anything seems unusual, don't hesitate to call me. Meanwhile you keep your eyes and ears open. If this young woman, Lola Morales, gets in touch with you, please let me know."

"Of course, it's just a matter of time. I'm sure she and Lenny will be back in touch. Thank you, Lieutenant."

"We need to be on our way. Thank you for giving Maria and her children a safe place to stay."

The *profesor* nodded his head in acknowledgement. The three of them went back to the living room, where Maria had laid out a few snacks.

Lieutenant Mendez offered his hand to Maria. "We must go, but we'll see you soon."

She took his hand slowly, with some shyness. "Lieutenant, can't you stay for salsa and chips?" Maria asked.

Mendez shook his head. "Sorry, next time."

The two policemen left quickly, waving to the children as the *profesor* let them out.

"We'll be in touch soon," Mendez said to Gilberto.

Mendez and Marin entered the car. "That woman

would make a very good wife for a policeman," Marin said.

"She's not bad looking either, Marin. Are you looking?" Mendez asked.

"Maybe, but I'd have to think long and hard about taking on all those kids."

"Yes, I'd give that some thought myself," Mendez agreed.

Marin looked at his lieutenant. "Boss, you never said you were in the market for a wife."

Mendez smiled. "I don't tell you all my thoughts," he said.

"Well, let me know if *Señora* Valdez is off limits."

"I think she would be astounded to realize there are two men out there interested in her. I think she was taken advantage of while living at the dump. I'm not sure she would trust another man," Mendez said.

"Well, I'm not sure I want a wife either," Marin concluded.

Mendez looked sharply at his Sergeant. "Don't take advantage of this woman, I won't have it."

"I wouldn't, Gus; I was just exchanging ideas with you."

Mendez pulled up in front of police headquarters. "See you tomorrow."

"You're not coming in?" Marin asked.

"I've got an errand to do. Tell them inside to send a couple of guys to pick up my car."

Marin exited the car and Mendez sped off.

Sergeant Marin knew that the lieutenant was

perturbed with him. He suspected Mendez was more than a little interested in Maria Valdez.

≳≲

*L*ater that afternoon, Jack ordered one of the enchiladas for which the *restaurante* was famous. After he finished eating he planned on walking over to Roy's video store and see if he had any new information. He took a long swig of his *cerveza* and dipped a chip into the salsa. Man, they made some real hot shit down here; his eyes stung and his nose dripped as he swallowed the salsa. He'd never heard of hot salsa growing up in Nebraska, let along eaten it. Vegas had a couple of Mexican places that served real hot food, but not quite this hot! He blew his nose just as his enchilada arrived.

Before he dug into his food he noticed a short, dark-haired man enter the *restaurante*. He wore a cheap suit jacket with a dark tie and wrinkled slacks. He took a seat with his back to the wall and glanced around the room before he looked at the menu. His eyes met Jack's and held them for a moment. Then he looked down as he opened the menu.

A cop, Jack guessed immediately. Just be cool, he told himself. He had no worries. No one knew he was here except Mr. Carscione. He continued to eat his meal, ordering another *cerveza*. His eyes could not stay away from the man seated along the wall. When he glanced over his way the man was staring at him. Shit! What was so interesting about him? Maybe because he was a *gringo?* Cops down here were always interested in *gringos.* Jack's reddish-brown hair made him stand out in a sea of dark-haired people.

He finished his food and motioned to the waitress to bring the bill. Leaving a nice tip for her, he stood up and walked by the cop, restraining himself from looking at him. He crossed the street and decided to walk down the alley to the back of the video store, so the cop wouldn't see him go in. He went round to the back and knocked. No one came to the door, so he knocked again, loudly.

"What the…" came from the other side of the door. "*Quien es?*" (Who is it?)

"Jack." He could hear a bolt slide back and the door opened.

Roy stood in the doorway. "Why you come to the back door?"

Jack explained he had lunch across the street at the Chihuahua Enchilada and he was sure there was a cop eating there too, and that he didn't want him to see him enter the video store.

Roy led Jack inside to his desk. "What does he look like?" Roy demanded.

Jack described him.

"Lieutenant Mendez. He was here a couple of days ago. Shit. Good thing he didn't see you come in."

"Why was he here?" Jack asked.

"He wanted to know if I heard anything on the street about Elmwood's disappearance," Roy said, not meeting Jack's eyes.

"How'd he know about Elmwood?"

"Elmwood was the boyfriend of the woman you whacked. Now he's disappeared and Mendez is looking for him, too." Roy grinned wickedly.

"Shit," Jack cursed under his breath.

"I may just happen to know where you can find him," Roy said.

Jack was taken by surprise. "What? Where the hell is he?"

Roy told Jack about Elmwood and three others coming to his place for illegal papers for the woman Lily Elmwood. "Neither of the two women was the one you are looking for. One was pretty, but a blonde; the other one was an attractive, overweight redhead. Ramon followed them to Santa Isabel and a boarding house. It's maybe an hour away." He gave him the directions, and Jack left out the back door. He walked around to the front and got into his late model car and drove out of the city.

After he discovered the four were gone from the boarding house in Santa Isabel, he headed to a small town south of Chihuahua, Los Campos. It was a tiny mining town not far from Santa Isabel. The old man at the counter said one of them mentioned Los Campos as they were leaving. If Jack staked out the town, Lenny would show up eventually. However, there wasn't a lot of time. He hoped he found Lenny and Lola in the next two days, otherwise he was screwed. He knew his boss Guido would have him removed from the job if he didn't produce results. That removal would be off the face of this earth.

He made the turn onto the dirt road and within five miles arrived in the village of Los Campos. There was a small *mercado*, a couple of *cantinas*, and a feed store. Parking in the back of the *mercado*, he walked down the main street, which was little more than a single lane dirt road, and stopped at one of the *cantinas*. He ordered a *cerveza* and took a table on the porch. This was a good vantage point to examine everyone who came into town.

After two days of camping out in his car, Jack was no closer to finding Lola. He was one pissed-off hit man with a giant headache from the constant anxiety. A plate of refried beans and rice was ordered. Jack gulped down his *cerveza* with three Tylenol, ate the food and headed back to Chihuahua. He needed to find a phone and call Guido. A couple days extension was all he needed. He wanted to check on the boys he had tied up in the warehouse, too. They hadn't eaten or drank any water for two days; he imagined they'd be ready to answer his questions now if they knew anything about the whereabouts of Lola Morales.

⋙⋘

The sky had turned a burnt orange with long sweeping brush strokes of yellow and pink intertwined like a Charles Reid watercolor. The distant mountains appeared in a blue-gray haze against the horizon.

Sherry and Lola were out back sitting beside the fire that Lenny had built. Lenny and Clint were inside cleaning their guns. Sherry lit a joint.

"What's happening with you and Clint? Are you in love?" Lola asked bluntly.

"I think so. I told him I'd stay with him if you decide to move on." Sherry looked into Lola's eyes for a response.

"That's wonderful, Sherry. I'm happy for you." Lola reached over and squeezed Sherry's arm. "I don't know what *I'm* doing. Lenny says he still loves me and wants us to be together. I'm so scared I can't make any long term decisions right now." She took a hit and passed it to Sherry.

"Yeah, I hear you. But you could do a lot worse than Lenny. He adores you. Remember Billy Jim?"

"Oh God, don't remind me of him. He seemed very sweet and protective of me at first. See — you never know how men are going to treat you after they begin taking you for granted."

Sherry threw the stub of the joint in the fire, and turned facing Lola. "You know, Lola, you're going to have to commit to something or someone eventually. It seems like you've avoided it all your life. It's about time for you to take some responsibility for your relationships and future."

Lola was astonished by Sherry's words. She took them inside herself and let them resonate.

Sherry had nailed her; that was for sure. Lola had avoided relationships with men all her life and she knew she needed to act like an adult in taking some responsibility for her actions.

"You are right about one thing, Sherry. I do have to stop running away. I've been running scared all my life, ever since my Dad sexually molested me. I've gone from man to man afraid of settling down and having a long-term relationship. When I met Billy Jim, I thought he was the one, but I was wrong about him. I'm afraid to trust Lenny." She clasped her elbows, hunching closer to the fire.

"You have to go with your gut instincts. He's been really good and understanding, especially since we brought his world to a stop and got his girlfriend killed."

"I feel really bad about that, and getting him and you and Clint in this serious jam. I blame myself for Gloria's death. Maybe I should just leave in the middle of the night and lead the killer away from México." Lola was rocking now beside the fire.

"That wouldn't solve anything. You don't need to go anywhere. We love you and want to help. You've got two strong guys, a faithful girlfriend, and four guns to protect you."

"And one experienced killer ready to eliminate me as quick as he can find me."

"It's four against one. I think the odds are pretty good," Sherry put her arm around Lola.

"We'll get out of this, I feel sure we will. But, time to grow up, girl." Sherry gave her friend a quick hug.

Lola looked at her friend. "You've been there for me, Sherry, ever since I've known you. I really appreciate your friendship. Thanks for being so optimistic when I've let myself get down in the dumps." Lola hugged Sherry back.

"You've been there for me, too, Lola," Sherry said with affection. "When I was allowing myself to be physically abused by Greg, you gave me the strength to leave him."

The screen door slammed and Clint came out to join them. "What do we have here, a mutual admiration group hug?"

Sherry extended her arms. "Sure. Come on in. It's free."

Clint put his arms around both girls and hugged them.

"Lola was getting a little down about our situation. I was just trying to cheer her up."

"She did, too. I feel better after getting a nice dose of positive attitude," Lola said, wiping a tear from her cheek. "Sherry helps me get my head on straight."

"I'm glad you two have it figured out. Lenny and I have cleaned all the guns, including yours, Lola. We're as ready as we'll ever be."

"I can see the hit man won't get any of us without a fight." Lola kicked some dirt on the coals as Sherry and Clint headed for the house.

"You're damn right," Clint agreed.

Overhead the sky was bejeweled with a million twinkling stars. The three of them stopped and listened. The wail of a coyote cut across the desert mesa like a call from the wild. Then several coyotes cried and yelped like harbingers racing across the sands for their kill.

⧓

Clint and Sherry were sitting in the back yard, smoking a joint. The sun was warm on his back and he took off his hat to get a few rays on his face. Sherry was sitting quietly in a camp chair beside him.

He hadn't fallen for anyone like he had for Sherry in several years. There had been a girlfriend now and then, but nothing serious. Not since his wife had left him for another guy. It was his own fault; he was so busy selling weed that he didn't see the warning signs. By the time he did recognized them, she was gone.

Sherry was an unusual woman. She was sweet, warm, uninhibited, and yet street smart and cautious at times. He liked the combination. He was glad he had asked her to stay with him. In a few months he'd ask her to tie the knot, make it permanent. He knew from his own experiences nothing was permanent. But he felt so good around Sherry, wanting to protect her, and at the same time, wanting to share his hardships, thoughts and dreams. She had agreed to stay with him, even if Lola and Lenny, or just Lola, moved on. He had no idea what was in Lenny and Lola's future or their plans. They hadn't shared their thoughts with him. But he could tell his friend was deeply in love with Lola. Probably he had been in love with her for years and didn't realize it. Why else would he choose a woman for a girlfriend who looked enough like Lola to be her sister?

Sherry reached over and clasped his hand beside their chairs. "Hey, a penny for your thoughts."

"I was just thinking about us, and our future. I think I'll stop selling; I don't need the money and I don't want to put you in danger."

Sherry's laughter danced on the afternoon air. "As if we weren't in enough danger, right now."

"True, but I'm thinking this will come to a head soon, and the four of us will win out!" Clint gave her a smile.

"I worry that Lola may get hurt before this thing is over."

"Not if Lenny and I can help it. We have enough fire power to bring this hit man down."

"I just want it to be over. I've had enough adventure for a lifetime. I want some quiet time for us so we can settle down and maybe have a child." Sherry sneaked a look at Clint.

Clint looked at Sherry, eyes wide in surprise. "What? Are you telling me something?"

"No, but I would like for us to have a baby. What about you?"

Clint scratched his chin. "I'd never thought about it. But it sounds like an okay idea." He leaned over and kissed her on the mouth. "How 'bout we go in and start practicing?"

Sherry giggled. "Okay, darlin', I'm ready."

⧓

$\mathcal{L}$ola and Sherry were in the back yard cleaning out the VW. Lola sat down on the stool beside the car. "You know, Sherry, I've been thinking. When I first ran away from home I spent several weeks eating at the Salvation Army soup kitchen in downtown Los Angeles. After a few meals I began helping prepare and dish up the food. The kitchen had a purpose and served the community by feeding those that were less fortunate. We should start a soup kitchen here. There's plenty of need for one. We could find a vacant building near the *barrio* and make dinner for the women and children. That way I could give back some of the good I have received."

"Not a bad idea, Lola. But do you think we might be a little strained financially with helping Maria and her kids?" Sherry replied.

"Yeah, I thought of that. I'm going to ask Lenny if he would help us. What do you think?"

"You mean help us with the money to supply the soup kitchen?"

Lola nodded. "He has said he would help us financially with Maria if we needed him to. Well, why wouldn't he help us with feeding the women and children of the *barrio*?"

Sherry whistled. "That's a big order, you know. We'd have to cook a bunch of food, and it would have to be Mexican."

"Why would it have to be all Mexican food? We could introduce casseroles and hamburgers, and a few other *gringo* foods. They might love it."

Sherry nodded her head slowly. "Hmm…maybe so. But what if Lenny refuses or says he doesn't have enough money?"

"It's just an idea I have in my head. If it doesn't happen, it wasn't meant to happen," Lola said.

Sherry smiled. "I like that philosophy. Why not look at life that way?"

"I try to, most of the time." Lola returned the smile. "Sometimes I get off course like with this hit man challenge that has me scared shitless."

"Why don't we wait to do anything concrete about the soup kitchen until this guy is off your trail and disposed of?" Sherry suggested.

Lola laughed out loud. "That's better than *my* being disposed of in concrete at the bottom of some lake by *him*."

"God, Lola, don't even joke about that! He's not going to put you in concrete. The four of us are going to get him first."

"Okay. But I could mention it to Lenny and see how he feels about contributing to the fund."

"That's up to you, he's your man."

"The worst he can say is no," Lola said.

That evening the girls made potato salad, fried chicken and apple crisp for dessert. When Lenny and Clint had pushed back their chairs and rubbed their stomachs, Lola brought the subject up.

She cleared her throat and seemed a bit nervous. "Lenny, ah…Sherry and I had a brilliant idea to open a soup kitchen for the *barrio* women and children, maybe feed them once a day. We thought of finding a vacant building somewhere near *the barrio* to set up. The problem is we would sure welcome some extra money, as our resources have quite a dent in them after helping Maria with her new place. I was wondering if you would consider adding some money to help us accomplish this." She leaned back in her chair and took a deep breath.

Lenny looked from Lola to Sherry to Clint and burst out laughing. "Of course I will. I told you I have quite a bit of money stashed and I think that would be a great cause to contribute to. How much are we talking here?"

"I have no idea how much it would cost," Lola said. "Maybe we could talk it over with *Profesor* Gilberto and see what estimate he comes up with."

"I would be happy to contribute, too," Clint offered, smiling at Sherry. "I think I told you both I have a lot of money saved from my various weed deals. I can't think of a better way to spend it."

"See, Lola. It's coming together. It's supposed to happen," Sherry said enthusiastically.

"The only thing I would suggest," Lenny interjected, "is to wait until we know what is happening with this hit man. We don't need to parade you out in the open for him by publicizing the soup kitchen and who's behind it."

"We wouldn't have to say who is behind it, would we?" Lola asked.

"No, but it may come out in the newspapers, who

knows?" Lenny replied. "And you would be very visible every day you are in the *barrio*."

"Lenny, I can't wait. We…I want to get started on this. My changed appearance will keep him from recognizing me if he passed me on the street. And I'll soon have my new identity. But thank you both for agreeing to help with the finances. Which of you is good at keeping books?" Lola asked.

Lenny sighed, "Okay, babe, I can see I'll have no rest until you get started on this new project, but we must be careful. Regarding the money, Clint is very good at making money grow. I've seen him parlay a few hundred dollars into a few thousand with his sales of marijuana," Lenny confided.

"Well then, if you agree, Clint, we will make you our banker and bookkeeper," Lola said. "We will each put in an amount, once it's determined what it will cost to open the kitchen, and Clint will take care of the money end of it."

Clint laughed. "You sure you three trust me with your *dinero*?"

"We wouldn't ask you to take care of the money if we didn't trust you, silly," Sherry quipped.

"It's settled then," Lola said, breathing a great sigh of relief. "We could all take a trip downtown and just look for buildings, couldn't we?" Lola suggested gently.

"We can look, but we really need to find a real estate agent to do this right," Lenny suggested.

"All right, how about tomorrow we take a trip into town?" Lola said excitedly.

"I'm game," Clint said.

"Sure," Lenny conceded. "If you two are hell-bent on doing this, Clint and I will help whenever we can."

Sherry squeezed Clint's hand. "Thank you, Clint and Lenny, for going along with us on this venture." She produced a deck of cards from the desk and they spent the rest of the evening playing penny-ante poker.

⋙⋙

*T*he next morning, the four of them left Diego's place early to go into Chihuahua to pick up Lola's I.D. papers. Lola tied a pillow around her waist, donned a long Mexican dress over it, and wore her horn-rimmed glasses, adding a straw hat to cover her hair. Sherry wore one of her new Mexican dresses and a straw hat also.

The day was warm, but a small breeze blew in from the west. Lenny drove Lola's Volkswagen so the four of them could go in one car.

They parked across the street from the video shop, in front of the Chihuahua Enchilada Restaurante. Sherry and Clint waited in the VW.

When Lenny and Lola entered the store, Ramon pointed them to the back. "Go in."

Lenny and Lola went behind the curtain. Roy was seated at his desk. He gestured for them to sit. "*Siéntese,*" he said. He handed a passport and a driver's license to Lola.

Lola looked them over. "*Sí, muchas gracias,*"

Lenny checked out the passport, too. "They look fine to me."

He turned to Roy. "Heard any more about the guy from Vegas?"

Roy shook his head. "*Nada.*"

Lenny gave him the remaining one hundred dollars, stood up, and Lola followed suit. "See you around, Roy." Lenny turned abruptly and led Lola out by the elbow.

Roy followed them out to the video store. "Don't you want to hear anything else?"

Lenny stopped. "What else?"

Roy decided to give up a piece of information to Lenny. "Uh…a cop, Lieutenant Mendez, came by asking me about a guy named Elmwood. Said he wanted to question you about Gloria. He asked me if I'd heard anything of your whereabouts on the street. I told him *nada.*"

"Okay. You told me." Lenny continued out the shop with Lola on his arm. They crossed the street and Clint and Sherry got out of the car. They entered the Chihuahua Enchilada Restaurante and took seats by the window.

When their food arrived, Lola felt much relieved. Her sore neck had stopped aching and her shoulders were relaxed. She was able to eat her meal with enthusiasm. The four of them talked about what might be needed to start a soup kitchen and what kinds of food they would prepare.

After Lola had finished her meal, she glanced around the room. She was about to take a drink from her Dos Equis when her eyes fell on a man in the back, sitting against the wall. He had reddish-brown hair and was looking around also. She nearly choked on her beer, but manages to put the bottle down on the table. The old tension returned as she realized who he was. The familiar feeling of fear gripped her like a vise across her skull.

Lola grabbed Lenny's hand under the table. "Lenny, I…think I see the…man. He looks like I remembered. Don't look now but he's in the back against the wall." Lola was whispering and looking down into her lap.

Lenny squeezed her hand. "Are you sure?"

She looked up at him. "No I'm not sure, but I think so." She spoke quietly. Lenny could see the beat of her heart in her temple.

"Look honey, just stay calm. He can't do anything here. I'm going to call this Lieutenant Mendez right now and we are going to tell him the situation. You stay here with Clint and Sherry." Lenny stood up and started to walk to the public pay phone.

Sherry had heard what had been said. She reached for Lola's hand and grasped it. "It's going to be okay. He won't do anything in a public place." Sherry sounded much more confident than she felt. By this time, Clint was also aware of the man in the back of the *restaurante*.

Lenny called and asked to be connected to the Chihuahua Police. Then he asked for Lieutenant Mendez and when questioned, said it was an emergency. He was told to wait. Finally Lieutenant Mendez comes on the phone.

"*Hola*, Lieutenant Mendez."

"Lieutenant, my name is Lenny Elmwood and I am

at the Chihuahua Enchilada Restaurante. My friend and I believe there is a killer looking for us and he is sitting in this *restaurante* right now."

Recognizing the name Elmwood, Mendez said, "Stay there. I'll be there in ten minutes." Both men felt the tension between them as electricity crackled over the lines before Mendez hung up.

When Lola dared to sneak a peek at the man in the back he was watching Lenny walk back to their table.

"God, he's watching us, "Lola whispered to Sherry.

"Just don't look at him," she said quietly.

When Lenny sat down the waitress asked if they wanted another *cerveza*. "*Sí, por favor*," Clint said, ordering four more *cervezas*. Lenny took Lola's hand again under the table and held it. "Don't sweat it, honey. We will get out of this, I promise."

Clint made idle conversation and so did Sherry. Lenny was sweating; large circles of wetness spread outward from under his arms. Lola fidgeted but Lenny held onto one of her hands.

Just as they were finishing their *cervezas* a short dark-haired man in a wrinkled suit entered the *restaurante*. He glanced around the room and spotted Lenny and Lola with two other people. Lenny lifted his hand slightly and Mendez noticed. He walked to them and sat down.

"I'm Lieutenant Mendez," he said softly. "No need to shake hands. Behave as if we know each other." With that, he slapped Lenny playfully on the back and leaned closer to him.

Lenny spoke quietly. "I'm Lenny Elmwood and this is Lola Morales. These are our friends Sherry and Clint. The two girls are visiting me from the states. It's a long story, Lieutenant. Lola witnessed a murder in Las Vegas over a year ago and the Mob is still sending out hit men to eliminate her. They screwed up the first time. There is a resemblance between Gloria Bernabe and Lola; you can see why Gloria was killed. The killer thought he was killing Lola." Lenny took a deep breath and leaned back in his seat.

Mendez scrutinized Lola. "I can't say as I see the resemblance but I assume you have changed your appearance, correct?"

Lola nodded.

While the three of them were talking, out of the corner of her eye, Lola saw the hit man get up. She elbowed Lenny and whispered, "He's leaving."

Mendez heard Lola and quickly glanced at the man. "I need to follow him; can you four meet me at Headquarters? Please wait for me there. Wait five minutes after I leave, then go to the police station."

When the hit man left the *restaurante*, Mendez jumped up and hurried to the back of the building into the kitchen and out the back door. He had meant to call for back-up and arrest the man as he left the *restaurante*, but he was moving before the lieutenant could make the call. Better to find out where he was going.

The four Americans waited five minutes before leaving Chihuahua Enchilada. Lenny drove them to the local police station which was only a five-minute drive from the *restaurante*. They explained to the clerk that Lieutenant Mendez had asked them to wait for him, and were ushered into his office.

Lenny smiled at Lola and smoothed the frown from between her brows. "We're going to be okay now. We got Lieutenant Mendez on our side."

≫≪

*J*ack's time was up and Guido had not heard from him. He called a new man to his office. This man did not know Jack Marchetti. Philippe Navarro spoke both Spanish and Italian and was very good looking.

"At your service, Mr. Carscione." The young man practically clicked his heels.

"Tomorrow I'll have my secretary book you a flight to El Paso, Texas." He handed photos of Lola and Jack to Philippe. "In El Paso, you will rent a car and drive to Chihuahua, México. Lola Raines is the target, and also Jack Marchetti. You two haven't met. He worked for me in the same capacity as you do, but he fucked up. This woman is still out there. Kill them both!"

Philippe nodded and said, "Yes, sir."

"I'm told the woman may be going by the name Morales. They are both in Chihuahua. Here are the names and addresses of two contact men who may be of some help, Juan Bolero and Roy Rivera. Once you have crossed the border in Juarez, make contact with this man, Raul DeSilva. He will provide you with a .45 automatic weapon with a silencer." Guido handed

Philippe a piece of paper with an address. "Don't come back without completing your assignment. I want this taken care of. This Lola Morales has lived a charmed life, so far. She refuses to go down." Guido knew that Philippe was a crack shot, as well as an ex-ranger who had worked undercover in Laos.

Philippe nodded.

"I expect the same high performance that you gave the U.S. government."

"Yes sir."

"Good. Be here at 8 a.m. tomorrow and pick up your ticket." Guido nodded in dismissal.

Philippe turned on a dime.

"Oh, and if you have a chance, before you kill him, tell Jack I think he's an incompetent asshole."

"Yes sir," Philippe responded without turning back to face Guido.

≋≋

*L*ieutenant Mendez left the *restaurante* by the back door and hurried through the alley to the front. He saw the man he was following cross the side street and go into the hotel on the corner. The policeman waited a few minutes before entering the lobby of the hotel. There were several people in the lobby and sitting at the bar.

Stepping to the desk he showed his police badge. "The man who just came in, what room is he in?"

The hotel clerk looked at his register. "Room 237,"

he said. The switchboard lit up and he excused himself to answer it. The clerk gave the caller an outside line for long distance. He turned back to Mendez. "He's making a phone call from his room."

Mendez nodded to him and put his finger to his lips. Taking the stairs was quicker; he suspected the man had taken the stairs also, as the elevator was still on the first floor. When Mendez quietly opened the stairwell door to the second floor, he looked up and down the hall. He found 237 easily; it was just down the hallway. Approaching the room he removed his .38 Special from the holster and stopped just to one side of the door. Laying his ear against the door he listened. He could hear a man's voice inside talking on the phone.

"But I want to talk to Guido. It's important." He was arguing with the person on the other end. "Hello, hello… damn!" he exploded as he slammed down the receiver.

Mendez holstered his gun, walked quietly back to the stairwell, returned to the lobby and made his way out of the hotel. He would arrest the gunman on the street when he left the hotel, rather than take a chance on hurting someone in the lobby. He made the decision that he didn't need to call headquarters. It was only one man. Mendez waited behind a large sign on the street. After some time the man had not come out of the building. Mendez called Marin at headquarters and gave him his location and instructed him to come at once.

⋙⋘

*D*amn that bitch secretary. She wouldn't let him talk to Guido, and she hung up on him. How dare she? But Jack was suddenly cold, as if he had taken a chill and was about to fall ill. His brow was sweaty and his hands were clammy. He'd better get that girl quick, or he was yesterday's news with his boss. He thought he'd recognized the guy in the *restaurante* as the guy in the photo he'd taken from Gloria's boyfriend's ranch. Neither girl resembled the target, but they could have altered their looks. The man with them was the policeman Jack had pegged earlier. He needed to get back to that rural town in the back country and keep it under surveillance.

He took the stairs and at the lobby hesitated. Deciding to go out the back door to the alley seemed wiser, since the cop was in the vicinity. He took the alley over a street where he had parked his car and headed toward Los Campos.

⋙⋘

*W*hen Detective Marin arrived, Mendez told him what had occurred. The two policemen entered the hotel and Mendez asked the clerk for the key to 237 and to keep everyone downstairs. They took the stairs two at a time, walked down the hall and drew their guns. Each took a position on either side of the door. Mendez listened and, hearing nothing, quietly put the key in the lock and turned it. Slowly opening the door,

Marin stepped in first. Clothes were strewn over the bed and floor. The door to the bathroom was open and both policemen could see it was empty, as was the room.

Marin checked the shower and found it empty, too.

"Damn," Mendez muttered. "He must have gone out the back."

Mendez and Marin closed the door to the room, holstered their firearms and went back downstairs to the lobby, returning the key to the clerk. Mendez shook his head and they left the hotel.

When Mendez arrived at headquarters, Lenny and Lola, Sherry and Clint were sitting in his office waiting.

"You've told me briefly the story of your last two years," the lieutenant said, taking a seat behind his desk. "Sounds like you've been on the run most of that time. Tell me in detail the entire story again, please."

Lola began at the beginning in Las Vegas, and covered her life up to and including coming to Lenny's ranch, and how they knew each other in the past. She told him of their imprisonment and escape from Juan Bolero.

Mendez smiled at Lola's explanation of how they escaped from the warehouse. She was a pretty ballsy woman to figure out how to get out of there, he thought, climbing through an air duct to the roof.

Lola also told of Clint's involvement and his initial arrangement for them to visit Juan. Lastly, she told him that the four of them were hiding out at Clint's uncle's place.

Lieutenant Mendez questioned Clint and Sherry and seemed satisfied with everyone's explanations.

"So Clint has given you a safe haven and now the four of you are staying there? Is that the situation?"

"That's it," Lola said.

"To relieve your mind, Juan has been killed, probably by the *gringo* from Vegas. He probably killed Gloria, too." Lieutenant Mendez glanced at Lenny. "I am sorry, *Señor* Elmwood. Now we have to make sure he doesn't connect with you," he looked straight at Lola. "I want you all to go back to Los Campos and carry on as before."

They left the police headquarters and headed out of town back to Clint's uncle's place.

Lola felt relieved with the lieutenant on their side. She felt better than she had since she found out another killer was on her trail in México.

※※

*L*ola and Sherry corralled the guys after breakfast. "We want to go into Chihuahua and find a real estate agent. *Profesor* Gilberto gave us a name and address," Lola spoke assertively.

Lenny put down his coffee cup. "Don't you think it's a little soon? I mean we just talked to Lieutenant Mendez yesterday. I'm not comfortable with you walking around the *barrio*."

"We thought you and Clint would come with us. It wouldn't be any different than going to the Chihuahua Enchilada Restaurante for lunch," Sherry put in her two-cents worth.

Lenny turned to Clint. "What do you think?"

"I think these girls are hell-bent on finding a place for their soup kitchen and they don't look anything like the two women that showed up on your doorstep a few weeks ago. What's the harm?"

Lenny sat in silence for a few minutes. "Okay. Guess I'm outnumbered. But we all keep our eyes peeled. We know what he looks like now. Anything unusual happens we hi-tail it back here. Agreed?"

Lola nodded and Sherry and Clint agreed. They got dressed and piled into Lola's VW and headed for the address of the real estate agent that the *profesor* had given Lola.

His office was located in a nice part of town. They knocked at the office door and a young man behind a desk motioned for them to enter. He stood up and immediately offered his hand. From their appearance he knew they were *gringos*. He spoke in English.

"*Hola*, I'm Miguel Aguerro. How can I help you?"

Lola mentioned *Profesor* Gilberto's name, introduced everyone and told him what they were looking for.

When Miguel heard what the girls were planning, he seemed genuinely surprised. "Let me look in my book and see what's available," he said. "You realize that you will need a *permiso* from the Department of Health before you can open this establishment?" He pulled a large volume from a desk drawer. "Please, have a seat."

"No, we didn't know that. Thanks for telling us. We are looking for a building that already has a kitchen unit so we can cook meals. And we would like to find something near the *barrio*. Perhaps a *restaurante* that has closed down. It doesn't have to be large," Lola explained.

After showing pictures of a few buildings near the perimeter of the *barrio* that included a kitchen unit, he pointed to one particular photo. "This one looks like we should go there and take a look. It seems to fit what you are looking for."

The photo showed a small wooden building with no windows in front. A sign dangled from a wrought iron balustrade connected to the roof. The paint was faded and peeling and the name of the *restaurante* was long gone.

"We don't mind having to fix it up; just as long as the rent isn't too high. What is the cost of renting this building?" Lenny asked.

"I don't know, it hasn't been occupied in several years. It may need a lot of work on the inside. But I think we can negotiate with the owner. Let's go take a look."

They all climbed into Miguel's station wagon and headed for the building. Miguel was right; it was on the edge of the *barrio*. Close enough for the women and children who lived at the dump to walk to it.

As he unlocked the rusty lock, Lola knew it would be the place for their soup kitchen. There was a large room, rectangular-shaped; big enough to set up tables for the people to eat on. It needed painting. The kitchen needed a good scrubbing and some paint on the walls, the sinks needed cleaning as well as the cupboards.

"Sherry I think this will do, fine. Don't you?" She whirled around, taking in everything in all four directions.

Lenny and Clint were of the same mind. "It needs some cleaning up but that's easy. It looks like the stove is in working order. We'll have to see when we have the gas turned on," Lenny observed. He found two large refrigerators and saw they were in good shape on the inside.

Clint inspected the back rooms for storage. "Plenty of space back here," he called through the open door.

The realtor, Miguel, went next door to a shoe repair shop and called the owner of the building. When the owner heard what the girls were planning for the building he said he would give them a big discount on the rent. Miguel returned to the girls and told them they could have it for 125 American dollars a month.

Lola and Sherry were elated. They hugged Lenny and Clint and Sherry gave a big hug to Miguel who stood by slightly embarrassed. But he knew it was given with good intentions and was happy for the four of them.

"Because you are a friend of *Profesor* Gilberto and because you are going to open a soup kitchen here I will waive my fee for finding this place. *Buena suerte señoritas*," (good luck) Miguel said.

Lenny pulled out his wallet and peeled off two one-hundred dollar bills and a fifty and handed them to Miguel. "Here's the first two months' rent, *señor*."

Miguel took the money and thanked Lenny. "*Gracias, señor*. Remember to get the permit."

"When can we start cleaning up, maybe tomorrow?" Lola inquired, looking from Sherry to Lenny to Clint.

Lenny laughed. "Yes, I think tomorrow is a good time to start. Are you free, Clint?"

"Your every wish is my command," he said, bowing to the two girls.

Miguel handed over the keys to Lola. There were two sets, and one to the back door. "I would suggest keeping the back door locked at all times. Once word gets out, you wouldn't want your food supplies ripped off."

All five of them in high spirits, they climbed back into Miguel's station wagon and headed back to the real estate office.

Lola felt very content with the developments of the afternoon. Her and Sherry's much-talked-about project was about to become a reality.

⋙⋘

*T*he next day Lola and Sherry drove to *Profesor* Gilberto's house and picked up Luisa and Federico for their first tutoring lesson. The *profesor* had left early for his office. Maria opened the door and greeted them. "*Hola, señoritas.* Thank you for picking the children up. *Muchacho, muchacha, estan listos?*" (Are you ready?) she called to the two children.

Luisa came out with a new school dress that Lola and Sherry has purchased for her. Federico had a new shirt and pants. Both had new sandals that had also been bought by the two women.

"Tomorrow we will pick up Rosa and Chado. Then the following day they will all go in together to their separate tutors," Sherry said.

Maria nodded when Lola translated as Sherry was speaking.

The children climbed into the back of the VW.

"Are you a little nervous?" Lola asked.

Rosa nodded but Federico shook his head.

"Why are you not nervous, Federico?" Lola asked.

"After facing a kidnapper who threatened to kill me and my brother, going to school is easy," he answered.

Lola and Sherry laughed at Federico's logic.

"I think you are already wise, young man," Sherry said, in English.

Federico nodded in agreement.

Lola and Sherry deposited the two children at *Profesor* Gilberto office where one of his students was waiting. The young college student had paper and pencils and a couple of beginning books on language set out on a table.

Lola introduced everyone. "The *profesor* will bring you home after your class. Be sure to wait for him here in his office."

The children nodded and the two women left the university and headed downtown to do some cleaning in the empty building.

PART III
Bonds

$\mathcal{M}$aria was so grateful for her new life and her two new American *señoritas*. However, the return of her boys was what she was most grateful about. She felt very indebted to Lieutenant Mendez and wished she knew in what way she could repay him. She didn't want to admit to herself that she found him attractive. In her most private moments before sleep overtook her, she would fantasize being in bed with him and, even more, a life with him. Of course, there wasn't the least possibility that she could ever be his woman. He knew she had been raped and forced to have sex many times when she lived beside the dump. A man like the lieutenant would never want someone like her for his woman. But she could dream about him and what it would be like to live in his fine house permanently.

Maria barely remembered how she started living at the dump. She was a teenager and her parents had both died. They had been poor, living off the land on a farm outside of town. But there was always food on the table. When both her parents died suddenly of influenza, she had to make some money. She had heard the city garbage dump held many treasures from wealthy households. She went there to sort through the garbage. That was the first time she was raped. When she returned to her farm home the next day, another family had moved in and told her she could not live there anymore. She went back to the dump, built a hovel out of cardboard and began her life as a garbage sorter.

Her parents had been religious and went to a local church, but when she visited the church and asked to see the priest, after many hours of waiting he finally sat beside her in the pew. When she told him about being raped, and losing her home, he told her to do her best in the place where she was living now. She found no help or sympathy from the church.

For many years Maria did the best she could, selling any small treasures she came across. Of course, the competition was ferocious, and if she found anything halfway valuable, she had to keep it on her person until she could sell it. All of her children were results of being raped. She never consented to any of the unions; however, she loved all her children. The American *señoritas* coming into her life was a godsend.

The house was quiet. The children were all asleep now. Her two oldest were tired from their first day being tutored. When they appeared at the door in the *profesor's* care, they were excited and full of everything that had happened to them. In rapid Spanish they told her about their lessons and the tutor and what a nice man he was.

Profesor Gilberto stayed for some of the news but said he had to get back to his office to correct papers.

Now the *profesor* was in his study reading and she had cleaned up the dinner dishes and was preparing for bed.

She looked at herself in the full length mirror in the bathroom. Her figure was still pretty good. Ample breasts that still stood up despite the nursing of five babies, a stomach slightly rounded and full, but not too full in the hips. Yes, she passed her own inspection. Would the lieutenant find her figure pleasing? She was sure she would never know. Even though she had detected a hint of interest at times when he looked at her, she was positive he would never act on it. He was a good man and would never take advantage of her as the other men had, who forced their way into her hut, raped her and then left. She wasn't sure who the fathers of her children were, it had happened so often. Finally she stopped fighting it, and just laid there until they left.

Maria slipped on her night gown, a pretty blue one that Lola and Sherry had given her. Quietly she climbed into bed so as not to awaken the girls, Ines on the other side of the bed and Rosa and Luisa on cots against the wall. *Profesor* Gilberto was so kind she could never repay him for giving them a safe place to stay. Even in her fantasies she could not have dreamed how her life had changed so dramatically and happily. Even if the lieutenant was not interested in her, she was the most fortunate of women to have been singled out by Lola and Sherry. As she fell asleep, the image of Lieutenant Mendez's lips came down on hers, blending into a long kiss.

≥≤

*L*ola and Sherry arrived at the run-down building on the edge of the *barrio* and parked the VW in front. Clint and Lenny would be down later to help. They went to pick up more cleaning supplies and the permit necessary for serving food in the soup kitchen.

"When is the electrician coming, Lola?" Sherry asked.

"Around eleven. He said he'd connect us to the city's electricity this morning." Sherry took some pesos from her pocket. "I want to give him some 'gift' money when he comes. They always do better work when they get a little compensation. I gather from Clint that the city wages are very low, so any extra money helps."

The girls started sweeping up the debris in the corners of the large room. In the kitchen area, Lenny and Clint were going to give the walls a coat of paint.

At eleven the city electrician arrived and connected the building to the city service. Lenny and Clint arrived with paint and more cleaning supplies. The girls spent five hours cleaning and scrubbing the walls in the main area. At noon several tables and chairs were delivered that Lola and Sherry had arranged for the previous day, as well as a few carts and shelves for the kitchen.

At 2:00 p.m. Lenny called for a break. "Let's go over to the Chihuahua Enchilada and have some lunch. Then we can come back and do more painting."

The four of them piled into the VW and headed for the *restaurante*.

They had a delicious lunch of chicken and corn enchiladas, rice and beans, *cervezas* and some *helado* for dessert. Then back to the building for more work.

The rest of the afternoon was spent painting and cleaning. The aluminum sinks and stove began to shine as Lola and Sherry put lots of elbow grease into the cleaning. By 7:00 p.m. the guys had closed the paint buckets and cleaned the brushes. Lola locked up the front door and they headed home for a cold dinner of left-over chicken and potato salad.

≋

*I*n between police calls Mendez found time to stop by *Profesor* Gilberto's house and see how Maria and the children were doing. He parked in front and knocked on the door. Maria opened it and smiled happily when she saw the lieutenant.

"*Hola, Señor Mendez.* Please, come in." She and Mendez conversed in Spanish. "The American *señoritas* picked up the children for their tutoring lessons this morning. The *profesor* will bring them home. Please, sit for a while," Maria said, closing the outer door.

Mendez hadn't meant to sit down, just to check on Maria. But he found himself following her into the living room and taking a seat on the sofa.

"Would you like a cup of coffee? Perhaps a cola?" Maria inquired.

Mendez shook his head. "No thank you. I just stopped by to make sure everything was all right."

Maria smiled again. "*todos esta bien, gracias, señor.*" (Everything is fine, thank you).

"I went by your apartment to make sure everything was okay there. Your landlady says she will keep an eye on it."

Again Maria thanked the lieutenant. "My landlady is very generous, a lovely lady."

Mendez stood up. "I must be going. I really can't stay." He took a card from his jacket pocket. "Here is my phone number. If you ever need anything, please give me a call. If it's an emergency, be sure to tell whoever answers who you are." He looked at her closely. "Can you read the numbers on the card, Maria?"

"*Sí, señor,*" she answered, taking the card from his hand. Their hands touched briefly and Maria felt a small jolt of electricity which she skillfully hid. But their eyes locked and she knew that he had felt it, too.

She walked him to the door. "Thank you for stopping by, *Señor* Mendez. *Buenas dias.*"

Mendez smiled at her and walked out to his car, climbed in and drove away. Humming a little tune, he was thinking how attractive Maria was and what a nice figure she had for having had five children.

⧓

*A*gain Jack headed out to Los Campos. Three days of surveillance hadn't produced either woman or Elmwood. An hour later he parked in back of the *mercado.* He walked inside through the back door and headed for the man at the counter in front. The store was empty except for the two of them.

He began to speak to him in English. "Sir, have you seen an American *señorita* in here recently?" He pulled Lola's photo from his pocket and showed it to the man.

The man looked at the photo and shook his head. "*No comprendo, señor.*"

Jack persisted. "Have you seen this woman," he said, pointing to the photo, his voice rising a few notes.

The man shook his head and walked into the back of his store behind a curtain. He understood some English but he pretended ignorance.

"God damn it!" Jack swore. He pocketed the photo and went out the front and across the street to the *cantina* to wait. He knew she was hiding somewhere near here; he just had to wait until she showed up again. Jack realized by now that Lola had probably disguised her appearance and it wouldn't be easy to identify her. Trouble was, he didn't have any more time.

Guido's refusal to take his call signified his time had run out.

⚹⚹

*L*ola and Sherry and Lenny and Clint had La Cocina de las Chicas (The Girls' Kitchen) in shape to open after a week of working every day. Lenny had painted the name on the sign and hung it outside the door. The main room was painted a pale blue and the kitchen was a mellow yellow. Yellow plastic place mats adorned every table. They wanted the place to have a homey atmosphere. Fresh flowers were placed on the mantel atop the old fireplace that had been rejuvenated. The girls had hung old bullfighter posters on the walls. The main room could seat sixty people with ten tables seating six per table. If they had more to serve, they figured by the time the second group was ready to sit down, the first group would be finished eating. If they needed more tables, Lenny said he and Clint could rustle up some extras.

Opening day fell on a Monday. The day before, the four of them had walked down to the *barrio* and handed out leaflets to tell the women to bring their children for a free meal the next day.

By nine o'clock there was a line down the block. The girls had just started cooking.

"What are we going to do? They are already lined up and we won't have the food ready for hours!" Sherry wailed, her usual calm demeanor deserting her at the moment.

"Relax. I'll go out and tell them. They can either wait in line or come back," Lola said, trying to calm Sherry.

Lenny went outside with Lola and she told the people gathered that the meal of the day would be served about 1:00 p.m. Several in line left, but about half of them stayed in place.

Lola and Sherry and Clint began making enchiladas, rice and beans. The girls had made several loaves of bread the night before in the large oven, and Clint and Lenny pronounced it excellent bread. Around noon, Lenny distributed the cut-up loaves outside to the people in line. He and Clint brought out a large barrel and a dipper filled with city water and paper cups. Lenny estimated there were approximately seventy-five women and children in line by one o'clock.

Lola and Sherry opened the doors and welcomed everyone inside. Lola told them they would serve until the food was gone. Next day she promised if they ran out of food, they would cook more.

By four-thirty, Clint figured a good one hundred had passed through the doors of La Cocina de las Chicas. They did run out of food, bread and all of the crackers in stock.

After baking fifteen more loaves of bread, cleaning up and doing all the dishes, Lola sat on a stool in the kitchen as Lenny came back from locking up. "I'm exhausted and hungry. What's for dinner, guys?" she joked.

"Looks like we have to take the girls out to eat," Clint said, laughing. The four of them climbed into the VW and headed for their favorite *restaurante*.

※※

*T*he next day the girls served spaghetti and marinara sauce, a dish many poor Mexicans had never eaten. Lola reasoned that when you are hungry, you will pretty much eat anything offered, and that was what the girls were counting on. This time they started cooking much earlier and finished feeding everyone by three o'clock. After cleanup, and more baking of bread, they got away by five o'clock.

"I think we need to buy the bread, Lola, from a local bread factory. It's too time-consuming and expensive to bake our own." Sherry offered this advice on the drive home. They started putting enough food for the four of them to eat for dinner in the fridge before they started serving. This made more sense than eating out every night.

Lola nodded. "I think you're right. Do either of you know where the bread factory is in town?" Her question was directed to Lenny and Clint.

"I do," Clint said. "Tomorrow I'll pay a visit and see what I can set up." He was trying to save the girls from having so many chores to do.

The next day while Lenny and Clint were away arranging for a daily bread delivery, Lola and Sherry were paid a visit by the local gangster.

A large, dark-haired man with tattoos on his arms walked into the back of the kitchen while the girls were cooking.

Sherry saw him first and she felt suddenly chilled in the 90 degree weather. She poked Lola to turn around. He stood in the door way for a minute and then entered and stood very close to the girls.

"My name is Ricardo and I came by to collect some insurance money from you." He spoke in Spanish but Sherry got the drift of his words.

Lola explained in Spanish. "We don't need insurance. We are feeding the homeless here. We don't make any money or profit at all. We are doing this on our own."

The man walked up close to Sherry. "Lovely blond hair, señorita," he said, as he reached up to finger a lock of it.

So quick even Sherry was taken unawares, Lola reached out and snatched the man's hand away from Sherry. "Don't touch her."

A sly smile flitted across his face. "Well, we have a lovely blonde and a spitfire Mexican *gringa*," he spoke derisively.

"You can't come in here and intimidate us, *señor*. We serve the community, and we don't want or need your interference." Lola spat back.

"That's very good. However, *señoritas*, everyone must pay Ricardo protection. Otherwise your kitchen could get torn up and your food taken away."

Lola understood that this man meant to do just that if he didn't get any money. "How much will protection cost us?" she inquired, pretending to acquiesce to his demands.

"I think fifty American dollars a month will do. But you must pay every month."

His smile made Lola want to slap it off his face. Instead she remained calm. "All right. Can you come back at this time tomorrow and we will have the money?"

"*Sí*, I will be back."Before he left he eyed Sherry again, making both the girls nervous. Sherry and Lola walked to the door and watched him hop on a motorcycle and take off down the street.

"My God, Lola, I thought he might pull out a gun and shoot you." Sherry pushed back her long hair from her face.

"I took a chance that he wouldn't really harm us,

at least not the first time. What he wanted was money and he thinks he's going to get it from us."

Lenny and Clint returned shortly and when they heard about the shakedown, Lenny immediately called Lieutenant Mendez on their newly installed phone.

The next day, Mendez and Marin were waiting in the storage room when Ricardo came through the back door.

Ricardo approached Lola. "Did you bring the money?"

"*Un momento*," Lola said. She opened the storage door and the two detectives stepped out with their guns drawn.

"Ricardo Alvarez, you are under arrest," Mendez said. Marin handcuffed the man and took him out to the car in back.

"You know him, Lieutenant?" Lola asked.

"Yes, he is a well-known small-time gangster. But no one has ever complained about his shakedowns. That is, until you two." He smiled at Lola and Sherry. "I may need both of you on my squad," he teased. "Looks like you two could clean up Chihuahua's streets single-handed."

"Don't jest, Lieutenant," Lenny said. "They may take it in their heads to join your police force as well as feed the hungry."

"You can relax," Lola said to Lenny. "We just won't put up with any interference with our feeding these women and children. Ricardo was an interference that we wouldn't tolerate."

Lieutenant Mendez spoke seriously now. "I'm leaving a policeman here for a week to be sure no one else shows up."

"Thank you, Lieutenant, but that isn't necessary. We have Lenny and Clint here."

"Yes, well, they were gone when Ricardo visited you. I'd feel better if I know he doesn't have someone working with him that decides to pick up where he left off."

"Okay, sir," Lola agreed.

The girls waved goodbye to Mendez and Marin as they drove out of the parking lot with Ricardo in the back of the police car.

≋≋

*P*hilippe had been delayed in his trip to México. When he showed up at Guido's office the next morning, Guido told him he needed to fly immediately to Reno to take care of a certain casino manager that was skimming. When he had taken care of that job, which had priority over the Mexican job, then he could catch a plane to El Paso and go on to Chihuahua by car.

Cindy, Guido's secretary, handed Philippe his ticket to Reno and he landed in Reno that afternoon, caught a cab to the center of town and then walked to the casino. He played the blackjack table for two hours, lost fifty dollars, played a little roulette and lost more money. It was nearly five p.m. by the time he did a surveillance of the back rooms and spotted the manager's office. He knew it would be locked from the inside, so no chance of getting in. He waited until six o'clock when he saw the night manager come on shift. The day manager, Ricky Wood, opened his office door to a knock by the night manager. Philippe followed Ricky out to his late model BMW and, just as he was unlocking his car door, Philippe shot him in the head. The silencer attached to his .22 made a sound like a sweeping broom on the paved parking lot. Ricky Wood slid down the side of the car. Philippe pushed the body underneath the BMW with his foot so it wouldn't be easily seen.

Walking back to the front of the casino, he hailed a cab to the airport and caught a nine o'clock flight to Vegas. He landed at McCarran Airport at 9:35 p.m., went straight to his apartment and picked up the phone.

He dialed a number and waited.

"Yeah?" Guido answered.

"Hello, sir. It's done. I'm home."

"Good. Come by the office in the morning and pick up your ticket for El Paso."

"Yes sir."

Philippe felt a sense of gratitude for his employer. He liked being appreciated for a job well done. He remembered his father, a minor gangster in Trenton, New Jersey, never appreciating him or anything he accomplished. He was a star on his high school football team, brought home good grades, but nothing seemed to impress his father. When he graduated, his father immediately put him to work in his end of the rackets, and he worked for him until he died. He was even 'whacking' his father's enemies, on his orders, in the years before his death, but Philippe never got a thank you or a kind word. In the end, his father lay dying at his feet, having been gunned down by a rival mob. Philippe could have taken him to the emergency room, but he walked away and let him bleed to death. That was what happened to people who didn't appreciate Philippe.

His mother was a different story. He stayed in New Jersey near her until she had to go to an assisted living facility. Her heart was very bad, and he knew she wouldn't live long. They visited together every evening and played cards or watched movies. Her last breath was taken in his presence. He'd loved her. She was probably the only person in the world that Philippe had ever loved. With her gone, he headed out west to Las Vegas with a recommendation from the man who took over his father's business. He had no trouble getting Guido's attention. He wore expensive suits, ties, kept a year-round tan, and ordered his shoes from Italy. He'd worked a year for Guido, but he felt his life was just beginning.

≷≷

*L*ola and Sherry's day at the soup kitchen became a routine. After the second week a young woman named Selena Jardin came in and offered to help with the cooking and organizing. Lenny and Clint did the shopping for groceries, and helped clean up every night.

Selena was a woman of thirty who had been a social worker but had to quit work to care for her ailing mother. When her mother died, she had a bit of money to live on and began looking for something to do to help the needy. She heard about La Cocina de las Chicas when she was in the *barrio*. How two Americans were feeding the hungry women and children of the city dump. She wanted to learn more about these two women so she dropped in one afternoon.

Lola and Sherry were behind the counter dishing out food. When Selena stepped forward Lola handed her a plate and looked up when the woman didn't immediately take it.

"Here is your food," Lola said in Spanish.

"Thank you but I'm not here to eat. I want to talk to you," Selena said in English as she stepped out of line so the next woman with two children could take the plates.

"Sure. Give us another hour and then we can sit down and talk," Lola said as she continued to dish up plates.

Selena took a seat at one of the tables and began talking with some of the women. What she heard during the hour she spent with them convinced her she wanted to help.

Lola looked up to take in Selena' appearance. She was tall for a Mexican; long dark hair tied in a pony tail and clad in American blue jeans and a loose fitting tee shirt. Her eyes were a deep green, which went very well with her honey skin and dark hair. She was very attractive but Lola could see she dressed down so her attractiveness didn't stand out.

When the line dwindled, Lenny and Clint took

over and Lola and Sherry walked over to Selena and sat down across from her. Sherry bought an extra cup of coffee and set it in front of Selena.

"What did you want to talk about?" Sherry asked. "By the way, sorry, I'm Sherry Brown and this is Lily Elmwood."

"Selena Jardin. I've heard many good things about what you are doing. I wanted to see for myself. I used to be a social worker and I'm looking for something helpful to do. I'd like to volunteer."

Lola and Sherry exchanged glances. "We'd love to have some help. Sherry and I are tied down here six days a week. If you could work with us a while and see how things are run, maybe you could relieve one of us now and then."

"I have a girl friend who might be willing to help. We could relieve you two at the serving counter."

"That would be wonderful. We are into our second week and both of us are tired already. If we didn't have Lenny and Clint to help us, I don't think we could do this," Lola confided.

"We didn't realize what a big job this is…to feed an entire community every day." Sherry agreed.

"Come back to the kitchen and meet Lenny and Clint. They will be very happy to hear you want to help. They've been telling us we work too hard," Lola said as they headed toward the kitchen.

Soon, Selena and her friend Marta were able to do a full day's work at the soup kitchen, including cooking in the mornings. Eventually Selena was able to take over the operations for a day or two at a time, giving Lola and Sherry some time off.

On their days off the four of them usually spent the time with Maria and the children, sometimes *Profesor* Gilberto and Lieutenant Mendez. Giving the lieutenant and Maria some time to be around one another was a good thing. They became very relaxed and laughed a lot.

The girls would bring food home from the soup kitchen or stop at their favorite *restaurante*, the Chihuahua Enchilada, and bring enough food to feed everyone at *Profesor* Gilberto's home. Gus Mendez became a frequent visitor to the *profesor's* home, visiting Maria and the children while still keeping an eye on her apartment to make sure no one was vandalizing it.

On one such evening, they were all assembled at the table in the *profesor's* dining room. The children were eating at the kitchen table.

"Is there any progress on finding the hit-man, Lieutenant?" Lola asked.

Mendez shook his head. "No, I haven't heard anything on the street; none of our snitches have heard anything either. But I have the small town of Los Campos under surveillance. He seems to have disappeared." Jack's gray Camaro had not been spotted and that was a source of disappointment to Mendez.

"I think Lola is getting a false sense of security since we opened the soup kitchen. I'm afraid she isn't as observant as she used to be. I check the parking lot every morning before we open the building, to make sure there are no intruders," Lenny confided to the group.

"That's a good thing, Lenny," Mendez agreed. "Sergeant Marin and I do the same thing on the street and around the building before you get there. Usually about 5:00 a.m. We are trying to keep all four of you safe."

Lola was surprised to hear that the lieutenant was doing this. "Thank you sir, for your surveillance. We appreciate it."

Mendez locked eyes with Lola. "No problem. We don't want anything to happen to you. A lot of hungry women and children depend on you now for their food. Another interesting thing I'd like to share with you. The violence in the *barrio* has gone down dramatically. I like to think it's because a lot of the residents have full bellies these days."

"I would think the men in the *barrio* are the instigators of violence. We don't feed them; in fact I've had to turn away several men who came to our dining room," Lola pointed out.

"For whatever reason, the climate is calmer; in fact, I don't believe we have ever seen this measure of calmness before," Mendez observed. "We can't know what's causing the drop in violence, but we want to believe your soup kitchen has something to do with it."

"I wish we could afford to feed the men too," Sherry said. "I hate turning them away."

"Perhaps that is something that can happen in the future," *Profesor* Gilberto suggested. "We can work on that problem."

⧓

*L*enny sat down on the side of the bed. He was hesitant about broaching the subject to Lola, but he decided to anyway. "Honey, I never got a definite answer from you, and I would like to know now. Will you be my wife and live here in Chihuahua with me?" His face betrayed the anxiety he was feeling.

Lola was taken unawares. They had finished a card game with Clint and Sherry, who had gone to bed.

"Ahhhhh…, I can't answer that right now, Lenny. I need to think about it."

"I sure would like to know so I can make plans."

"What plans?"

"Wedding plans." He looked up into Lola's face.

She avoided his eyes. "I can't right now. And anyway, I wouldn't want anything fancy…just something simple…if we get married."

"What is this 'if' bit?" he said, more sharply than he meant to.

"Lenny, please. Don't press me right now. I'm trying to keep together this soup kitchen and I don't want to be distracted with thinking of a …wedding."

"Our wedding would be a distraction?"

Lola realized immediately her mistake. She had hurt Lenny. "I didn't mean that the way it came out. Please let's don't fight. I can't give you a definite answer right now. Please accept that."

Lenny laid his head back on the pillow, closed his eyes and didn't say anything.

"Please don't be angry with me. I just need some time to think about it." Lola undressed and turned out the lights. She'd screwed up and hurt his feelings. She hadn't meant to hurt him. God, he was so sweet and good to her. Climbing in beside Lenny, she turned toward him and laid her hand on his shoulder but he lay rigid under her touch, on his side turned away from her. She rolled over with her back to him and that's the way they fell asleep.

⧓

*J*ack had been in Chihuahua three weeks—two weeks longer than Guido had given him to hit his target. He knew he was on someone's hit list now!

He lounged on the bed in the run-down hotel, a bottle of whiskey beside him. The ashtray was brimming over. Butts were scattered on the table top and on the rug beneath the table. He had moved to a cheaper hotel a few blocks away from the first hotel.

The guy at the first hotel had maybe 'made' him, he thought. His behavior was different and he didn't like the way he watched him, so Jack had moved. He couldn't find the woman he was supposed to kill. He was damn angry! His hours were numbered if he didn't find her. Maybe he should light out for Puerto Vallarta or Acapulco and take a different identity — start over. Roy could give him a new I.D. This anger that took hold of him was unshakable and a slowly-encroaching fear was spreading within his mind. His throat was slowly closing down like a drawbridge and he could hardly eat. A throbbing in his head bothered him most of the time, no matter how much booze he drank or pills he took.

He knew he should be staked out all the time at Los Campos so he wouldn't miss the woman when she appeared in town. But he couldn't get up the energy to get in his car and do the hour's drive. His life was turning to shit. He'd screwed up the kidnapping of the boys. When he drove by the warehouse he saw the cop car and knew they'd been found. They would talk and tell the police what he looked like, what questions he asked. He should have killed them instead of leaving them there. The police would know now he was looking for Lola Morales, and they would know he was a hit man. She would have been warned and probably went further into hiding. He would never find her. Shit!

Finally Jack climbed off the unmade bed and took a shower. He dressed carelessly, pocketing his gun, money and I.D. Leaving the hotel, he headed for his car across the street. He needed to eat something but he couldn't go back to the Chihuahua Enchilada Restaurante because the cop the girl was talking to had seen him and probably had his picture posted. He headed out of town and stopped at a small *cantina* on the highway, ordering rice and beans. As he ate, his heartburn kicked in and he had sharp pains under his ribcage. He belched several times and tried washing everything down with a coke. Having only consumed half of his meal, he left some money on the table and went out to his car, heading for Los Campos.

⋙

*L*ola, Sherry, Ines, Rosa and Luisa were playing cards at the table in Clint's uncle's place in Los Campos. Lola and Sherry had decided to bring the girls out for a day since it was the boy's day for tutoring and the *profesor* would take them to and from their lessons.

"I have the Old Maid," wailed Rosa, throwing it down, knowing the game was over and she the loser.

"Don't feel bad, dear," Sherry said, "It's just a card game. We'll play another time and you may win that time."

Luisa comforted her younger sister. "We have all had the Old Maid at one time or other."

Rosa and Luisa's English was improving almost daily because of their tutoring lessons. Ines still spoke Spanish, but the older girls translated for Sherry.

Lenny came in from the backyard. He pulled Lola and Sherry aside and said, "Do you girls think it was wise to bring these kids out here?"

"I don't think we're putting them in any danger" Lola said. "The lieutenant says the hit man hasn't been seen lately. And we know the lieutenant has a man watching us."

Lenny didn't respond. He had been distant lately; Lola sensed his disappointment. He didn't smile as often. She knew he was bothered by the fact she had remained silent concerning their wedding.

He hadn't been down to La Cocina de las Chicas for two days, begging off saying he had some errands to do. Clint had faithfully helped them, and Selena and Marta took over working the kitchen two days a week. That helped immensely, too.

Sherry and Lola started a middle-of-the-day meal so they could take the girls home early. Lola had been cooking the beans all morning. The rice was easy and the guys would grill the chicken outside.

When the meal was ready, Lenny and Clint sat down at the picnic table on the back porch while the girls and Lola and Sherry brought out the food.

≋

*T*he next morning Lola and Sherry drove into Los Campos for some tortillas and powdered milk. Lola parked Betsy on the outskirts of town and they walked the two blocks to the *mercado*. Lola had her tent dress on, the pillow tied around her waist, and her horn-rimmed glasses. Sherry had her hair covered and also wore a long Mexican dress. The idea was to not stand out as *gringas*.

Jack was sitting across the street when the two women walked into the market. Neither of them looked like the photo he had of Lola. They were dressed in traditional Mexican dresses. But they were the women he'd seen in the *restaurante* with the guy in the photo, Lenny Elmwood. He watched them pick out a few items, pay for them and then leave the store. They turned back down the way they had come. He waited to see which tarpaper shack they turned into, but they kept walking until they disappeared around the bend in the road. Jack jumped up and hurried down the dirt road until he got to the bend. He saw them pulling away in an old, beat-up VW Beetle. Roy had said the four were in a Beetle with Arizona plates. He ran back to the parking lot behind the market and climbed into his car. Damn, he thought, he'd almost lost them. By the time he made it around the bend in the dirt road they were still in view. He stayed well enough behind that they wouldn't become suspicious. When the car slowed and turned into a long dirt drive, he went on by, stopping down the road behind a large cactus and a clump of rocks.

He got out and hid behind the cactus. In the distance a small adobe house stood alone with no other houses nearby. He pulled his binoculars from his backpack and focused on the Beetle with Arizona plates, then noticed a truck and a red Corvette in the back yard by an outbuilding. The two women got out of the VW and took the bag of groceries inside.

Jack lit a cigarette and contemplated his next move. Roy said there were four of them. Who the hell were the others? He knew one was Gloria's boyfriend, Lenny Elmwood. One was Lola, his target, but he wasn't sure which woman. Who were the other two? And why were they all together? Christ, he'd have to take out all four, and he wouldn't get paid for any of them. He could wait until nightfall and take them by surprise while they slept. Or he could rush them right now. Probably better to catch them asleep.

As the sun set, he saw the four leave the house by the back porch and sit around a small campfire that one of the men had built. They were smoking something they passed, probably a joint. He smiled to himself. It was coming together after all. He'd 'whack' them tonight and be out of México by tomorrow morning and on a flight from El Paso to Vegas.

God, he'd be glad to get back to the bright lights of Glittertown. That's what he called Las Vegas. He'd been lucky to fall into the right crowd after he'd moved to Vegas. To a hick kid from Nebraska, Vegas seemed like paradise.

≷≶

Lenny passed the joint to Lola. "See anything unusual in town?" he asked her.

She shook her head. "No, we weren't there ten minutes. We parked on the edge of town like you suggested, walked to the *mercado* and then came right back."

"Right after you returned, I saw a late model car pass by," Clint said.

Lenny looked alert. "Why didn't you say something? People around here don't drive late model cars."

"I was planning on telling you just like I did now," Clint said with a grin. "Means we have to do guard duty tonight."

Lola blew out the smoke and coughed. "Oh God, will this ever be over?"

Sherry put her arm around Lola's shoulder. "Try not

to worry. We will all do our part to protect you."

"I'm worried about all of us, not just me," Lola added.

"Me too," Clint said. "If the hit man tries for Lola, he plans on killing all of us."

Lenny stood up and looked off to the south and then to the west. The sky had turned a gorgeous deep pink with layers of yellow and mauve. But the sunset was lost on Lenny. "I think we ought to go in. We're easy prey out here. Don't hurry, just walk slowly." He kicked dirt over the coals and reached for Lola's arm. The four of them headed for the back porch.

Once inside, Lenny went to his backpack and took out his .45. Clint did the same. Lola dug in her bag and found her .32 Beretta. Sherry reached for the rifle standing in the corner.

"This represents our fire power," Clint said, looking down the barrel of his gun. "Somehow I think this guy will try to sneak up on us. Maybe try to kill all of us while we sleep."

Lola had visions of Tony having his throat slit in his bed. She shuddered at the thought.

"I'll take the first watch," Lenny said.

"I'm sitting up with you," Lola said as she slipped her gun in her jacket pocket.

"Wake me at 2 a.m. I'll take the early morning watch," Clint said as he and Sherry headed for the bedroom.

Lenny locked the back door to the porch and the front door. He checked all the windows, making sure they were locked. Some had been nailed shut. Turning out all the lights, he placed a chair in a corner of the living room where he had a good view of the front and back entrances to the cottage. Lola sat down beside him on a cushion on the floor. "Want something to drink?" she offered.

"How about some water?"

Lola got up and went to the kitchen. She brought back two glasses of water. "I'm so sorry I brought this trouble down on you, Lenny. I wish I had thought it out more carefully before deciding to come here to visit you."

"We can't go back, honey. Let's just take this a day and night at a time. I'm committed to getting us out of this. Besides, I'm glad you did come. Otherwise we might never have seen each other again." He leaned down and kissed her lips. But they didn't make love. Lenny wanted to be totally focused on guard duty.

The two of them fell into a silent reverie. Lola thought of what her future might hold if she stayed with Lenny. She knew she loved him, but she didn't know if she would be content to live with him here always. He had suggested if she didn't want to stay in Chihuahua, they could move to someplace else like Acapulco or Puerto Vallarta. She had always been partial to Zihuatenejo, on the Pacific coast south of Acapulco, having spent a few weeks there after she and Lenny had broken up.

Lola knew she wanted to continue the soup kitchen for a while to be of service to the *barrio* community. However, she wasn't sure she wanted to do it permanently.

Her mind moved back to the subject of marriage. Did she want to be tied down? She wasn't the fickle kind; she knew she wasn't interested in anyone else and probably would never be as long as she and Lenny were together. These questions kept playing hopscotch with her fear of the moment. The mind can be a terrible thing when you are trying to remain focused on staying alive. Gradually her grip relaxed on the gun in her pocket and she curled up next to Lenny. Her eyes closed and her breathing slowed.

※※

Sherry and Clint lay down on the top of the bed quilt, completely dressed. Both were quiet. Sherry didn't think they'd get any sleep but just to rest was good for them. She desperately hoped the four of them would be alive in the morning. Nothing like this challenge had ever occurred in her life before. Just staying alive would be a huge accomplishment. She had full confidence in Clint and Lenny's abilities to defend her and Lola, but there was still a lot of fear about the off chance that one of them might get hurt or killed.

She cuddled close to Clint's side. Having found this unusual and caring man, especially after losing Ronnie, she didn't want to have anything happen to Clint and their happiness. Sherry knew instinctively that there wasn't much any of them could do about the situation except defend themselves. Realizing they really had no control, just choices, helped her keep a measure of calmness. She finally relaxed and settled beside the man she had chosen to spend her life with.

Clint lay very still, listening to the night sounds out on the desert. Sherry lay beside him, quiet. He heard the call of a coyote and the reply. He heard the wind rustling over the top of the roof, and the cholla wood falling to the ground in the back yard. Having been raised in the desert he recognized the ripples and moans that swept across the barren mesas. His native heritage allowed him to be nearly at one with the elements. Somewhere out there Clint felt there was a man with a gun bent on killing the four of them.

≷≷

Jack chewed a stick of Juicy Fruit gum and checked his gun to make sure it had a bullet in the chamber. He wanted a cigarette badly, but knew it would be foolish to advertise his presence to anyone who might be awake. The smell of cigarette smoke traveled quite a distance.

This job was finally coming together. He'd whack the four people in the cottage and start driving to El Paso, tonight. There was no need to go back to the cheap hotel. Calling Guido from the airport would be a good idea, so he would know the job was done.

Damn, this woman had been a difficult hit. You'd think she had the fuckin' angels on her side. Even Guido mentioned she was difficult to take down. Now he had her in his sights. Well, almost. He'd do a head shot to make sure she was good and dead. The other three needed to be whacked so there were no witnesses.

Jack wondered if he was maybe losing his grip. Had he lost the cutting edge of his skill? He had never before screwed up finding his target. When he got back to Vegas, he'd brush up on his tracking skills.

It was time. He took his silencer from his pocket and screwed it in place on the end of his gun. Moving from behind the rock formation, hunkered-down like a guerilla fighter, he hiked across the field to the back of the house. Nearing the structure he slowed his pace as the crisp soil snapped under his soft-soled shoes. He crept carefully around the edge of the house to view the back yard. The corner of the tool shed would give him a complete view of the house before he entered.

≋

Lieutenant Mendez parked his car behind an outcropping on the dirt road leading to Diego's cottage. He walked a half mile until he saw the house up ahead on the right. The moon was full, giving him good light. Checking his watch, he saw it was past midnight. He decided to take a shift to watch the girls and give his men a break. He saw one of his detectives drive away a few minutes ago. He had signed in on the surveillance sheet at headquarters that he would do the midnight shift. He had nothing pressing to do and he cared about the welfare of Lola and Sherry, as well as Lenny and Clint.

Cutting across a field Mendez, came up in back of the cottage. All seemed quiet; the lights were off. It looked as though everyone was asleep.

Mendez crept to the side of a small tool shed and slid down the wall, resting on his haunches. He had a view of the back door. He crawled to the corner of the building and peered around a rotting wooden beam. The wail of a lone coyote cut across the mesa. An answer came quickly as another howled back. Mendez shivered in the cool desert evening. He saw a shadow materialize suddenly and turned his head to look over his right shoulder. An excruciating pain spread across the side of his head. Blackness enveloped him.

≶≶

Suddenly Lola felt a touch on her shoulder, and she jumped. Lenny's hand patted her softly. Beneath his breath he uttered, "Shushhh…"

She lifted her head and looked at Lenny. He was pointing toward the back. He crept out of the chair and crawled a few feet behind the couch, pulling her with him.

He spoke very softly in her ear. "I heard something on the porch."

The hair stood up on the back of Lola's neck when she heard a soft cracking, perhaps of someone's knee or ankle joint. "Want me to go get Clint?" she whispered.

"No time," he whispered back.

She saw Lenny's .45 in his hand so she pulled her

gun from her pocket and held it beside her, muzzle down.

They heard the lock on the back door being picked. Very quietly it opened and a figured slipped inside. Lola could see a dark shape moving stealthily across the room toward the bedroom. She felt a shiver like ice slide down her spine. Her hands were clammy and stiff. The gun nearly slid from her grasp. She tightened her grip. The vague smell of cigarette smoke was in the air.

Lenny moved to the end of the couch and fired a shot at the intruder. Lola's legs were not moving well she was so scared. She scrambled to the opposite end of the couch. The black shape moved toward her and Lenny. The intruder fired back in their direction. The sound was muffled, like a hiss from a cat. She didn't bother to think; she just reacted, firing at the source of the gunfire. Compared to the gunfire from the killer, her gun and Lenny's made a deafening noise. In a flash, the intruder moved to a corner of the room, hunkered down and began firing back. Lenny kept firing at the shooter until suddenly Clint came out of the bedroom with his .45 pumping hot metal across the room. Apparently Clint's bullets connected. They heard a groan from the corner. Lenny stood up and fired more bullets into the killer, moving closer to him as he continued to shoot. The smell of gunpowder was overwhelming. Lola felt a sneeze coming on. She stopped it with her finger pressed against her nostrils. The killer fired at Lenny and Lenny cried out and fell to the floor. Clint fired again. She heard the killer fall into the end table and the sound of breaking wood. Lola was beside Lenny in a second. She covered him with her body. Suddenly, the full moon slide from beneath a cloud and shone in through the windows, like a beacon. When Lola turned her head she saw the killer sprawled a few feet from Lenny on his back, gun still in his hand. His eyes were open and he blinked. Lola raised her gun and shot him once in the face. He died with his green eyes still open.

"Lenny, honey," she cried out. Sherry was beside Lola and they both began searching Lenny's body for the wounds. Lola found blood on his thigh. She grabbed the scarf from her neck and tied a tourniquet around his upper thigh.

"Is he hurt bad?" Clint asked, walking toward the killer on the floor.

"I don't know yet," Lola was checking Lenny's body for blood.

Clint put a finger to the throat of the killer then removed the gun from his hand and laid it on the table. He looked at his friend, Lenny.

"Lenny. Can you talk?" Clint asked.

"Yeah," Lenny said.

"Is the thigh the only place he got you?"

"Yeah," he repeated.

"We need to get him to the hospital. The nearest one is Santa Isabel." Clint picked his friend up from the floor with the ease of a weight lifter. "Sherry, get the keys to the truck. Bring it around to the front. We need to take him now. Lola, you drive the VW and follow us. We'll clean up this mess later."

Sherry ran out the door and brought the truck to the

front. They loaded Lenny in the passenger seat. Lola ran out back to the VW and found Lieutenant Mendez lying on the ground beside the front bumper. She leaned down and touched his face. His eyes flew open.

"Where are you shot?" Lola asked the lieutenant. She could see blood on the outside of his jacket.

"Chest," he gasped. "Can you call the police? My car and radio are down the road. Ask for Sergeant Marin. Tell him Mendez is down."

"I will, but we need to get you and Lenny to the hospital," Lola said. 'We'll head for Santa Isabel. There's a hospital there."

"Just a few miles away," Mendez said, his voice getting weaker.

Lola called loudly to Sherry and Clint. When they appeared around the corner of the house Lola called out, "Come help me get Lieutenant Mendez into Betsy. He's been shot, too."

Between the three of them they loaded Mendez into the front seat.

"Once we get to the hospital I'll call your Sergeant, Lieutenant," Lola said.

But there was no reply from Mendez as he had lapsed into unconsciousness.

Clint pulled the truck up to the VW and Sherry hopped in. He took off and Lola slipped behind the wheel of the Beetle and followed Clint to Santa Isabel.

At the hospital both vehicles pulled up to the emergency entrance at once. Sherry ran inside and told the nurse there were two gunshot victims that needed medical assistance immediately. A couple of orderlies with gurneys ran out and transferred Lenny and Lieutenant Mendez to the gurneys.

Lola hurried after Lenny. She leaned down and kissed him on the lips. "I'll be right here waiting for you," she assured him.

"Thanks, honey." Lenny said, smiling for the first time.

"I promised Lieutenant Mendez I would call his headquarters once I got him to the hospital," Lola said as the three of them followed the gurneys.

"I wonder how the killer got the draw on him," Clint said.

"I can't imagine. It's happening too fast," Sherry said.

"We'll get the answers when Mendez is conscious," Clint said. "Right now you'd better get in touch with the Chihuahua *Policia* and let them know what happened to their lieutenant."

When Sergeant Marin came on the line, Lola explained that Lieutenant Mendez was in the Santa Isabel Hospital, and that he had been shot in the chest.

The Sergeant immediately wanted to know who was calling.

"This is Lola Morales. We are at the hospital and my friend Lenny Elmwood has also been shot and is in the hospital." She agreed to wait for him to arrive.

Lola hung up and sat down next to Sherry. "I'm exhausted," she said.

"Me too," Sherry agreed. "Boy, I never saw you so

fierce as when you shot the killer in the face." Sherry looked at Lola with new respect.

"I hope I'm not in too much trouble for killing that man. I was so angry that he had shot Lenny, I hardly remember shooting him. We were fighting for our lives." Lola rubbed her eyes.

"Somehow I don't think anyone, including Mendez, will hold it against you that you killed a hit man from Las Vegas," Clint said laughing. "Besides we all shot him."

"Do we know he *was* the hit man, Clint?" Lola asked.

Clint pulled a wallet from his jacket. "I took the liberty of taking this out of his hip pocket."

He opened it and they looked at the license. Clint read, "Jack Marchetti, 102 Andover Place, Las Vegas, Nevada. He was thirty one years old." They saw a picture of a reddish-haired man with green eyes in a suit and tie. "Kind of too bad; he didn't have a chance to really live a life." Clint mused.

"He sure took the wrong damn job when he came after Lola," Sherry blurted.

Lola shivered as she looked at the photo carefully. "He was the other man who killed Tony," Lola said in hushed tones. "You need to turn this over to Lieutenant Mendez."

"Yeah, I'll give it to Sergeant Marin when he comes to the hospital."

"They're both dead, now, girl. You're home free." Sherry laughed and gave Lola a big hug.

"I hope so," Lola uttered softly.

≋

*L*enny came out of the anesthesia and asked for water after the bullet had been removed from his thigh. The nurse wheeled him into a room and said, "In a little while. There's someone who wants to see you." She smiled as she ushered in Lola.

Lola came over to the bed and kissed Lenny tenderly on the lips. She noticed his pallor matched the whiteness of the sheet.

"Honey, will you lick my lips, they won't give me any water and I'm so dry."

Lola laughed and kissed him gently, licking his lips. Then she wet a towel in the glass of water and squeezed a little over his mouth.

"Ummm...Manna from heaven," Lenny murmured.

"The doctor said your thigh will heal fine."

"Lucky me. That damn shooter almost got me in the stomach. If I hadn't moved at the last minute I might not be talking to you right now, or worse, I may not have been able to father any babies," Lenny joked.

"What possessed you to march toward him firing? You looked like John Wayne going after the outlaws," Lola said, laughing.

"I was so pissed off; I guess I thought I was invincible."

"I don't think I've ever seen you so mad," Lola said laughing.

"Nobody messes with my woman," Lenny said, his eyes beginning to drift downward.

"I need to go see Lieutenant Mendez. He was hurt pretty bad. I'll be right back." She glanced back at Lenny as she left the room. His eyes were closing.

Lola walked down the hall to Lieutenant Mendez's room. When she entered there was a dark haired man sitting next to the lieutenant's bed. Mendez's eyes opened and he gave Lola a small smile.

"How are you doing, Lieutenant?" she asked.

"I've been better. Thank you for getting me to the hospital in time. The doc said if I'd lost any more blood it would have been too late."

Mendez was hooked up to an IV and was receiving blood. Lola came to the side of the bed and patted his hand. "I'm happy we got you to the hospital in time, but I have to tell you, I shot and killed the hit man. I think Clint and Lenny both shot him, but I shot him in the face after he shot Lenny." She looked down at their hands. "I can't say I'm sorry, Lieutenant. He was sent by the Mob in Vegas. They have been hunting me for over a year."

"You've had a pretty adventurous couple of years, young lady." Mendez gestured toward Sergeant Marin. "Thanks for calling him. He was worried about me when I didn't show up for work. First time I didn't call in. That's what I get for being so predictable." He smiled at Sergeant Marin.

"Lenny's down the hall. He took a bullet in the thigh. He's going to be fine. But Lieutenant, there is a dead man on the living room floor of the place we were staying."

"I figured he was dead, since you weren't," Mendez said dryly.

"Oh, Lieutenant, you joke about it, but I have been terrified for so long. I didn't know how much longer I could have evaded the killer."

"If you ever want to take up law enforcement, let me know. I could use a fierce police person like you on my team," Mendez said.

"I don't think I would be a good police person. It's different when you're fighting to stay alive. And when I saw Lenny shot, I killed him, without any remorse," Lola said.

"As far as the body is concerned, Sergeant Marin has already called headquarters and they are taking care of it." Mendez frowned as he moved his shoulder.

"Lieutenant, will I be charged with killing that man?" Lola asked, her voice wavering.

"I was thinking along the lines of you being shot dead and this information being communicated to the Las Vegas newspapers. That way the word will get back to the Mob that their hit man was killed in a gun battle after he killed Lola Raines-Morales." He smiled as he saw the look of amazement on her face.

"You'd do that?" Lola said.

Mendez nodded.

Lola leaned down and kissed the lieutenant on the forehead. "You are a dear man, to save my life in this way."

"Turnabout is fair play. You saved mine. Of course you'll have to get some new I.D. And you'll have to live the rest of your life under a new name."

Lola grinned, and glanced at Sergeant Marin. "Uh…Lenny and I went to a man in the *barrio* and got me some new I.D. recently. When you met us in the *restaurante* we had just picked up my new drivers license and passport." She looked a little embarrassed.

Mendez laughed softly. "I was going to recommend Roy. He does most everyone's I.D. in Chihuahua."

"Yes, he's the one. He told Lenny and me that a hit man was looking for us. Apparently the hit man showed a photo of me to Roy and he said that was not the woman who came with Lenny for I.D. papers."

"I can see you've changed your appearance a lot. Good for you. You may need to stay a redhead."

"I can do that," she said.

"By the way, what name did you get your new I.D. in?" Mendez asked.

"Lily Elmwood."

"You took Lenny's last name? Does that mean you two are getting married?"

"I don't know, Lieutenant. But he said he'd loan me his name for as long as I needed it." Changing the subject, Lola asked, "by the way, can you tell us what happened in the back yard? We didn't hear any shots."

"I was camped out by the shed. I didn't hear or see him sneak up on me. He must have struck me in the head with his gun, and then shot me in the chest. You didn't hear a shot because he used a silencer." Mendez rubbed the side of his head gently where he had a large knot.

One of the nurses came into the room. "I think you two better let the lieutenant get some rest. He's talked long enough."

Sergeant Marin and Lola stood up. "Thank you so much, Lieutenant. I can never repay you for giving me back my life," Lola said, her eyes moist.

"Hey, you'd better come and see me again. I'm not through talking to you." Mendez said as the two them left.

"Oh I will," Lola said.

In the hallway, Sergeant Marin took her arm. "I need to get an official statement from you. Can we go down the hall?"

"Sure," Lola said. They went to the waiting room where Clint and Sherry were sitting.

"How's Lenny?" was Clint's first question.

"He's going to be okay," Lola said. "So is Lieutenant Mendez."

Sergeant Marin proceeded to get statements from all three of them as to what exactly had occurred and in what order. When he was finished he said, "Lieutenant Mendez says none of you will be charged with anything. As far as the police in Chihuahua are concerned, a hit man from Vegas was killed in a gun battle with police after he had killed Lola Raines-Morales."

Clint and Sherry looked at Lola. "Wow that makes everything work out fine. Lola's life is saved and the Mob in Vegas will think she is dead," Clint said. "But what about the body in my uncle's place in Los Campos?"

"Don't worry. The Chihuahua police have already been there and removed the body. My regrets that they didn't clean up the mess. We did take the guns that were left there. But you will get them back. It is just normal procedure."

Clint took out the wallet belonging to Jack from his back pocket. "Sergeant, I took this off the dead man. I wanted to be sure he was the guy from Vegas."

The sergeant looked straight into Clint's eyes. He opened it and counted out five hundred dollars in the wallet. "Thanks for turning it over to me. You could have cleaned it out and we would never have known."

"I don't need his money. Besides, it has blood on it." Clint smiled.

"Thanks, again, Clint," the sergeant said sincerely.

"Lola and Clint and I are free to go?" Sherry asked the detective.

"That's right. In order for the lieutenant's plan to work, Lola Morales is dead. And the hit man died in a gun battle with police."

"I think we ought to get some breakfast, Sergeant," Clint said. "Care to join us?"

"*No, gracias,*" Sergeant Marin smiled. "I need to stay here and talk to the lieutenant when he wakes up. You go ahead. I'll see you over at the Los Campos place later."

When the sergeant walked away, the three of them left the hospital and went across the street to a small *cantina* for breakfast.

"I think Sergeant Marin is more worried about the

lieutenant than he wants anyone to know," Sherry said astutely.

Clint agreed.

"That may be, but I think the lieutenant will recover quite nicely. Of course he will need some care when he gets home," Lola replied.

Once she sat down in the *cantina*, Lola felt weak from exhaustion. Her hand trembled when she picked up her water glass. She was so grateful that Lenny was going to recover and that Lieutenant Mendez would recover also. Thank God for large favors, she thought. What she was going to do with her life and her new identity was something she hadn't discussed with Lenny or herself. She had a lot of talking to do in the next few days with Lily Elmwood.

≫≪

*L*enny finished his lunch and pushed his tray down on the end of the bed. He had been thinking all morning about his and Lola's future. He hoped she would marry him but he wasn't at all sure that would happen. Lola had always been independent and had avoided marriage all her life, probably because she abhorred her parents' relationship and her mother being in denial about her husband's sexual molestation of their daughter.

He felt that Lola loved him, and he had always loved her, having never found a woman quite like her. As far as staying in Chihuahua, if Lieutenant Mendez did what he proposed—leak information to the Vegas police that Lola had been murdered by a hit man—then they could return to his ranch and live there with Lola's new identity. However, he wasn't sure if Lola wanted that. She hadn't talked to him about her plans for the future. All of these confusing thoughts roiled around in his head until he acknowledged a headache. He scooted down in bed and decided to sleep on all of it.

⋙⋘

*M*endez finished his lunch and contemplated how he would arrange the news of Lola Morales' demise to appear in the Las Vegas papers. Having a contact with the Vegas Chief of Police was helpful. He would call and tell him that Lola was killed by the hit man and that he, in turn, was killed in a gun fight with the police. He'd ask the Chief to make sure the papers got the information. That should do it. The Mob would find out and that would be the end of her being hunted.

She and her friend Sherry seemed to be a pair of fine young women, the way they befriended Maria and her family. He would do all he could to help them.

Maria was something else that had been on his mind for a while. She was also a fine looking woman and so conscientious. He had been attracted to her from the first, but he never mixed police business with pleasure, at least not until now. A widower for many years, the thought of a family again sent small waves of happiness through him, like the thrill of winning a great prize. Maria was a prize, even though she didn't read or write.

Her qualities were so much more valuable than book learning. The five children would be able to further themselves in their lives, thanks to Lola and Sherry providing the tutoring for them.

Mendez leaned back and snuggled down in his pillow. His mind settled; his entire being felt as though he was a much younger man. He felt stirrings down below that had been dormant for a long time. Thoughts of Maria did that to him.

※※

Sherry rubbed her eyes and climbed carefully out of bed so as not to wake Clint. She went into the kitchen and started coffee. Soon, Clint appeared in the doorway, stretching, his tee shirt straining against his biceps.

"Hungry?" she asked.

"Sure am."

Lola walked into the kitchen in blue jeans and tee shirt. "Hi. I went into town and picked up some farm eggs." She placed the bag on the counter.

"Lola, you need to wear your disguise, even now," Sherry scolded.

"I will wear the glasses and hat when we go out, but Lily Elmwood is on a diet and pretty soon she will be back to her usual weight. I don't think it matters now that the hit man is gone. By the way, I thought we all needed a hearty breakfast after last night."

The three of them had gone back to Diego's place and cleaned up the mess after the police had taken down the Do Not Enter sign. They had scrubbed everything spotlessly clean, working late into the night, disposing of the old rug with blood stains, and burning the broken and bullet-ridden furniture. After several hours of hard work they all fell into bed. Sherry and Clint took the bedroom and Lola slept on the porch.

"After breakfast I'm going to the hospital to see Lenny. What are you two up to?"

"I thought we'd go to my place and clean up. No reason why we can't move back in now," Clint said, with enthusiasm. "I'm kind of missing my place and Sherry wants to fix it up."

"Okay," Lola was thoughtful. "I'll come over and help after I see Lenny. I was wondering if you two would help me clean up Lenny's ranch. There is a lot to do, but between us we could probably get it done in a day. Maybe tomorrow?"

"Of course, we will," Sherry said, looking at Clint for agreement.

"Certainly, and by the way, you are welcome to stay with us at my place until Lenny gets out of the hospital. No need to stay at the ranch by yourself," Clint added.

"Thanks, Clint." Lola blew him a kiss.

They sat down to a breakfast of eggs, potatoes, toast, bacon and coffee. Selena and Marta were taking over the soup kitchen today. Afterwards the three of them left for separate destinations.

※※

*L*ola arrived at the hospital around eleven a.m. and went immediately to Lenny's room.

He was sitting up having his lunch.

Lola gave him a long kiss on the lips. "I've missed you, Lenny. I'll be so glad when you are home."

"Me too, honey."

"Have you heard from Lieutenant Mendez down the hall? How is he doing?"

"I went down to see him this morning in a wheel chair. He's recovering very quickly. But he will be here longer than I will. When he gets home he will need some care before he can return to work."

Lola bit her lip in thought. "I was thinking, Lenny, maybe Maria could move over to Mendez's house and take care of him. What do you think?"

"What about the kids? Do you think he could handle five kids in the house?"

"I don't know but I think we should ask him, anyway. He could pay Maria just as easily as he can pay someone else to come in and care for him. And the children have tutoring three days a week. They wouldn't be around all the time."

"Now that the hit man is dead, she and her children could move back into their boarding house. The kids could stay there and Maria could go during the day to care for Mendez," Lenny mused.

"I think I'll ask him before I say anything to Maria. I feel sure she would want to help him. Then we have to consider if *Profesor* Gilberto will wait a while longer for Maria to return to work cleaning the archeology building at the university." Lola was busy mapping out the lives of her dear friends, which now included Lieutenant Mendez since he had given back her life. "Mind if I walk down to see the lieutenant? I'll be back in a jiffy."

"Go ahead, honey. I can see you aren't going to be happy until you get this worked out."

Lola flashed him a big smile which Lenny returned.

Down the hall Lola entered the lieutenant's room and found him eating his lunch. He had a nurse assisting him.

"*Buenas dias*, Lieutenant," Lola greeted him.

"*Buenas dias*, young lady. So good to see you." He pushed the spoon away from his mouth and the nurse gave him a look of disapproval. "I'm finished, *gracias*, *señora*. I have a visitor now."

The nurse scolded him with an outburst of rapid Spanish, but retreated, smiling at Lola, in spite of being sent away.

After the nurse left, Lola leaned down and kissed Mendez' forehead. "I want to thank you again for saving my life and for everything you have done. If it weren't for you, I would probably be dead now. I have too much to do, Lieutenant, to die just yet."

Mendez took Lola's hand and held it. "I was only doing my job, but I admit from the moment I saw your picture, I wanted to find you and keep you safe. There are so many young women here in México who go missing and most are never heard from again. I'm very glad you weren't in that category."

Lola took a seat beside Mendez's bed. "Lieutenant…"

Mendez interrupted her. "I think we know each other well enough that you could call me Gus if you want. I would like that."

Lola smiled, a tightness grabbing at her throat. She feared she would choke up. She had never let any man, except for Lenny and Billy Jim, get close enough to her to affect her emotions. This man, who could be her father in age, was getting through her barrier.

"All right, Gus. I have a proposition for you…don't say a thing until I'm through. The doctor told me that you will need care when you return home. I was thinking that Maria could come over during the day and care for you. What do you think? You will have to pay someone to do this, so why not pay Maria?"

Mendez was silent thinking over the proposition that Lola had presented. He thought she was a pretty savvy woman, perhaps even sensing his interest in Maria.

"What about Maria's day job at the university?" Mendez asked.

"I need to talk to the *profesor* about that. I was hoping he could do without her a couple of weeks until you are back on your feet."

"If Maria wants to do this, I will pay her very well, and of course, if the *profesor* agrees. You certainly are an organizer, *señorita.*"

"Thank you, Gus. You are a very easy man to get along with."

Mendez held up his hands. "Hey, I know when I'm

outclassed. You have it all worked out."

Lola gave him a shrewd look. "I suspect you aren't unhappy with my suggestions."

Mendez's eyes twinkled. "You are probably right, Lily."

Lola was startled to hear her new name. "Guess I need to be called that for a while so I can get used to it. Lenny, Sherry and Clint still call me Lola."

Mendez' demeanor became serious. "Listen, you must forget your given name. Don't slip up. Always use your new name in public. If you do this in private, it will come easier."

Lola stood. "Okay, boss. I get the message. Now I'm off to help Sherry and Clint clean up his place; it's been vacant for several weeks. Then tomorrow we are cleaning up Lenny's ranch. It's in pretty bad shape and there is a lot of work to do there."

"When will Lenny be released?"

"In a couple of days. I want everything clean when he goes home."

"You come back to see me, now, *comprende?*"

Lola laughed. "Of course, Gus. I'll l be back. I'll even bring Maria if you want."

Mendez' face took on a slight pink hue. "Well, okay, if she wants to come."

Lola realized how transparent the lieutenant was.

⧓

*T*he next morning the three of them were at Lenny's ranch, cleaning up the mess from the searches by Juan's henchmen. Several pieces of furniture were beyond repair. The men who invaded the house broke up some of the furniture looking for God knows what. Clint and the girls carried pieces of furniture out to the back yard and built a bonfire. The couch and chair were moved to the garage in Lenny's work space. Lola and Sherry scrubbed and waxed the tiled floors in the living room and dining room. After everything was cleaned and the fire burned out, the two girls got in Betsy and drove to the best furniture store in Chihuahua. Clint stayed at the ranch, re-hung the screen door and fixed the holes in the walls, spackled and painted over them.

The girls picked out a new couch and chair of soft beige suede, a lovely glass coffee table, an end table, and some bright pillows for the couch. A large blue and brown pattern rug was purchased for the living room area. An 8½ x 11-foot rug was purchased for Diego's place in Los Campos to replace the blood-stained carpet they had to throw out, plus several pieces of furniture that had been destroyed by the shootout. A Mexican blanket with red, blue and yellow stripes to throw over the back of the couch was also chosen for Lenny's living room. Lola paid cash for the items and the owner happily agreed to deliver the goods that afternoon. The rug and furniture that was destined for Diego's place would be delivered next week when Sherry and Clint would be there. In a moment of spontaneity Lola bought a new blue bedspread and matching sheets for Lenny's room. Lenny was coming home from the hospital tomorrow and Lola wanted the house complete.

After the furniture truck, which had followed the girls home, delivered all the items and left, the girls and Clint placed the furniture in a different pattern than before. When they finished, the large open room looked like a page from a House Beautiful magazine.

"Lenny will like this, don't you think?" Lola asked Clint and Sherry.

Sherry nodded. "I think he will be overjoyed. He isn't expecting this."

"You don't think he'll be upset that I chose the décor for his house, do you?" Lola asked Clint anxiously.

"I think Lenny will be very happy at the changes. After all he asked you to be his wife and live in this house. As his wife, you would naturally want to have a say in the décor."

Lola bit her cuticle. "We aren't married yet. I don't want to jump the gun."

"Stop worrying. He'll love it. It looks so peaceful and cozy." Sherry patted her on the shoulder.

They decided to wait until Lenny was home tomorrow to toast and christen the new room. Clint said he would buy a bottle of Champagne. They piled into Clint's sports car and drove to their favorite place, the Chihuahua Enchilada Restaurante, for dinner.

≳≲

*L*ola pulled the VW up to the front entrance of Vista de Pajaro and Clint parked his red sports car right behind. The cactus garden was in full bloom; *ocotillo* flowers spilling over their stalks welcoming the owner home. Pink blossoms from the prickly pear cactus were scattered in between the *ocotillo*.

Clint hurried over to the VW to help Lenny out. The hospital had given Lenny crutches and he managed to walk, slowly. Clint helped his friend up the steps of the porch. Lola and Sherry were standing inside the open door.

When Lenny crossed the threshold he saw the living room, bright and clean, filled with all the new furniture. He took in the spotless new rug and banished a momentary vision of the last time he'd seen his living room in a shambles with much of the furniture broken.

"Holy cow! Is this the right house?" He grinned. He knew the person behind this, but he asked anyway. "Who may I thank for this lovely gift?"

Lola put her arms around his neck and hugged him. "Welcome home, darling. I hope you like it. Sherry and I picked it out. If there's anything you don't like, we can exchange it for something else."

"Hey, I love it. How much did this new look cost me?"

"That's the best part," Clint said. "It's Lola…Lily's gift to you."

Lenny shook his head in amazement. "You don't have to bear the cost of this, honey. I'll pay you wherever you spent."

Lola shook her head. "Absolutely not! This is what I wanted to do. I brought this entire disaster down on you. I am responsible for getting your girlfriend murdered, for the destruction of your house, for you getting shot, and I wanted to do something to help make up for it." She looked suddenly serious. "Of course, I can't bring Gloria back; I'm so sorry about her loss."

"Sweetheart, I appreciate your tender heart, but Gloria didn't have a chance once you bounced back into my life. Thank you so much for this lovely gift." Lenny hobbled to the new sofa and sat down slowly, put his crutch on the floor, arranged a cushion along the couch and brought his injured leg up. "Might as well break it in."

"As long as you don't break it *up*. . ." Clint joked.

They all laughed at Clint's humor.

"We have a nice lunch for you and Clint that Sherry and I prepared this morning," Lola said. The girls went into the kitchen and brought back a steaming tray of chicken enchiladas and rice. Placing it on the table laid out with four blue placemats and blue napkins, Lola spooned a portion onto Lenny's plate. "Come sit down. Lunch is served."

Sherry appeared from the kitchen with a large bowl of salad and Clint brought in the champagne and four champagne glasses.

Lenny hobbled over to the table and the other three joined him.

"Wow, I should come home from the hospital every day." The spicy aroma of baked enchiladas and cheese swimming in the hot sauce permeated the room.

Clint opened the Champagne with a whoosh, and filled the four glasses, foam sloshing over one rim. He wiped it with his finger.

They held up their glasses and Clint made a toast. "Here's to long and fulfilling relationships," he said.

"I'll sure drink to that," Lenny said.

The four of them dished up their plates and began eating. Lenny and Clint dug into their food like starving laborers. Sherry and Lola exchanged smiles.

When they had finished eating, Clint pulled a joint out of his shirt pocket, lit it with a Zippo, took a long drag and handed it to Lenny. The joint was passed around twice and when it became too short, Clint pinched it with his fingers and stuck the roach back into his pocket.

Sherry held up her glass. "Here's a toast to good friends. May life's fortunes shine on us from now on."

They all clinked glasses again.

The sun streamed through the back windows, casting a rosy glow over the rainbow-striped blanket thrown over the new couch. All was well at Vista de Pajaro.

≋≋

Lola and Sherry knocked on Maria's door and Rosa opened the door.

"*Señoritas, pasen, por favor,*" Rosa said.

Maria was at the stove making stew. Ines and Luisa were sitting in the window seat looking at a book.

"*Señoritas, como esta?*" Maria asked.

"*Muy bien, gracias,*" Lola answered, as she deposited the bag of groceries on the counter.

Ines, Rosa and Luisa rushed over and hugged Lola and Sherry.

"*Gracias,*" Maria said.

Maria gestured for the girls to take a seat at the table. She came over and sat down with them.

"First, Maria and children," Lola explained in Spanish, "I must tell you something very important. From now on, you must call me or refer to me as Lily. This is my new name. It's a protection for me against anyone looking for Lola. *Comprende?*"

"*Sí, Señorita Lily,*" Maria answered. She explained to the children that they were also to call her Lily from now on. The girls giggled and nodded their heads.

"Where are the boys?" Sherry asked.

"Out somewhere. They are more careful now about people and their surroundings," Maria replied.

"This is good," Lola said. "Maria, we have an idea. Lieutenant Mendez will be coming home from the hospital soon and he needs someone to care for him. We were wondering if you would do this. He will pay you to care for him. And *Profesor* Gilberto says you can work at the university on the housekeeping crew in the afternoon. He will make sure the children are returned home after their school lessons."

Lola noticed that Maria's face flushed a deep pink.

"*Sí, señorita*, I would be happy to care for Lieutenant Mendez." She clasped her hands together in front of her apron.

"The lieutenant will be coming home soon and we will pick you up on the morning of his return so you can have his bed made up, and tidy his house. Is that okay?" Lola asked.

Maria nodded.

"Gus is putting out the word in Las Vegas in the United States that Lola Morales was killed here in Chihuahua. You must always remember that Lola is dead. Your new friend is Lily," Lola added. "Gus is a pretty special guy."

Maria agreed, nodding, again turning a lovely shade of rose.

"We have errands to do in town, today. Tomorrow we will come again and take you all out to lunch. It's your day off, *sí*?" Lola asked.

"*Sí*," Maria answered.

"Can we take the girls back with us to the ranch? We'll bring them home after dinner," Sherry spoke up.

"Of course, they will love to visit your place." Maria turned to the girls and told them to wash their face and hands in preparation to go with Lily and Sherry.

Ines, Rosa and Luisa hurried down the hall to the bathroom chattering excitedly as they left the room.

"*Gracias, señoritas* for taking the girls. They will be good, I promise."

"We aren't worried about the girl's behavior, Maria," Sherry said. "We adore them. They are always good girls."

Maria put her hand on Lola's arm and pulled her back down in the chair. "*Señorita* Lily, she said, a concerned look on her face, "is the lieutenant hurt badly? You never told me about his injuries."

"He is very much on the mend; the wound in his chest is nearly healed. Fortunately the bullet missed his heart. He probably won't want to stay in bed all day. He can get up but he will need assistance in fixing meals and doing his laundry, things like that," Lola said.

Maria nodded, understanding what her role would be as a caregiver. "I will clean his house too. Hopefully he won't be like *Profesor* Gilberto, not wanting me to move anything to dust."

Sherry, Lola and Maria had a good laugh about what a neat freak the *profesor* was. The girls streamed back into the room and stood before Lola and Sherry.

"We are ready, *Señoritas* Lily and Sherry," Luisa said in English, emphasizing the word, 'Lily,' amid giggles from all three.

"*Bueno*," Lola said. She stood and took Ines' hand in hers. "*Vamonos*," she said, giggling with Ines. Sherry and the other two headed out the door.

Maria walked them to the outside door and watched as the three girls piled into Lola's VW and they all drove away.

≫≷

$\mathcal{P}$hilippe had landed in El Paso, Texas and rented a late model car, heading for the border. At customs he was asked if he had anything to declare and he told them *nada* (nothing). His fluent Spanish and good looks plus an extra twenty dollar bill got him extra polite treatment from the customs officers. Once over the border in Juarez he went to his contact, Raul DeSilva, and picked up a .22 automatic with a silencer.

He headed south, driving through the rolling hills of the State of Chihuahua. As soon as he finished this assignment he would stop at the border town of Juarez, and find a pretty *señorita* to spend a night with. He'd always loved Mexican women. In fact, the tall cold-hearted bitches in Vegas that worked as call girls couldn't hold a candle to *Latinas*. The last time he was in Juarez he remembered the house he'd gone to and the girl he had paid for. He'd return to the same bordello; hopefully she was still there. There was never time for relationships; he was too busy working for the Mob. When he wasn't working on an assignment, he was working out in the gym.

Upon returning to Vegas he must remember to send his sister in New York some money. She was recuperating at a clinic up-state, drying out again from her alcohol problem. He wished she would take some responsibility for her life, but it was easier to rely on her big brother. Their parents were both gone, so he looked after Lori as best he could. Maybe he should ask

Guido for a week off to visit her. Lori always fell back into the old crowd, the guys that hung out all night at bars. She made the worst choices in men. Marrying two worthless drunks hadn't taught her a thing.

Their mother had been a level-headed, smart, school teacher, who brought up her two children to be career-oriented. Lori had barely held down a job in her thirty years; once, she worked as an usher at a theater in New York, and later on, as a waitress. But neither job had lasted long. Being the only relative she had left was somewhat of a burden, but Philippe had tried to help her. His career was demanding and unpredictable as to where he might be sent at any given time. However, the money was very good and he could afford to pay for his sister's clinic fees.

A month ago he had dropped in unexpectedly on Lori in her New York apartment, and found her dead-drunk at one o'clock in the afternoon. He'd immediately arranged for her to be transferred to the clinic and had stayed with her for one entire day. That was all the time he had to devote to her then. If this assignment went well and quickly he could ask Guido for some time off.

Suddenly a truck appeared over the next rise, going very fast. The truck was on the wrong side of the road. He could see the driver with a bottle to his mouth partly obstructing his vision. Philippe knew the truck was headed straight for his car. Before he could do anything to change direction, the large vehicle plowed into the front of the late model car, sending it plunging over the bank and down a deep ravine.

The last thing Philippe thought as he fell to his death was that he wouldn't have the illustrious career with the Mob that he had planned.

※※

*L*ola stepped into Gus's room and saw he was asleep. She sat down beside the bed and waited. Five minutes later he opened his eyes and saw her.

"Hello, young lady. What are you doing here?"

"You told me to come back and visit you. So I'm here."

Gus wiped his hand across his brow. "*Que de nuevas?*" (What's new?)

Lola updated him on Lenny's return home and that he was recovering nicely.

"He's hopping around on one leg; I can't keep the man down," she said laughing. "We've arranged with Maria and the *profesor* that she can come in the mornings to care for you once you're home, and in the afternoon she will go to the university and work with the house-keeping crew. The children will be taken to and from their tutoring classes by Sherry, me or the *profesor*."

She updated Gus on their progress with La Cocina de las Chicas and their good luck in finding a woman, Selena Juarez, who wanted to help by volunteering a couple of days a week.

"And she has a good friend, Marta, who helps her, so she is able to run the soup kitchen when we aren't there."

"It sounds like you have everything under control," Gus said, sitting up in his bed. "I should hire you as my private secretary to keep my records straight. Whenever I want to find something I filed, it takes me a long time to locate it. I'm not a good record keeper."

"Perhaps when I have time I'll pay you a visit at your office and straighten up your files. Would the Police Department permit a private citizen to do that?"

"I think I can arrange it to be all right, Lily," Gus responded with a smile. "Thanks for that great suggestion. Maybe once they are in order I can keep them that way."

"Maria says she would like very much to care for you."

Gus blushed visibly. Lola grinned at him.

"You just need to recover enough to come home. Has the doctor said when you can be released?"

Mendez shook his head. "Not yet; maybe in a couple of weeks. When I tell him I'll have care at home he'll probably let me go sooner."

Lola stood up. "I'll be back tomorrow. I think the whole gang is coming. Federico and Chado want to see you, too. Are you up to that?"

Mendez squinted back the emotion creeping into his eyes. Moisture formed at the corners. "Sure. That would be great. Bring the three girls too."

"I was going to, if it's okay with you. We don't want you to experience too much excitement and set your recovery back." Lola said jesting.

"No fear of that. I'm ready now to leave."

"Do you think the doctor will talk to me?" Lola asked Gus.

He nodded. "I think so. Just tell him you're a family member. They always talk to the families."

Lola leaned down and kissed Gus on the forehead. "See you tomorrow."

"Hey, I'm going to get used to those kisses on the forehead. They better not stop."

Lola laughed as she left the room.

Down the hall she saw the lieutenant's doctor sitting at a desk writing his reports. Lola stopped at his side. "*Hola*, doctor, I am Lily Elmwood, a member of Gus Mendez' family. Could you tell me when he can come home?"

The doctor looked up. He was young for a physician. "He will probably be ready next week. His chest wound is healing nicely. His rate of recovery has been very rapid for a man of his age. Just check with the nurses next week as to what day he will be released."

"Thank you, doctor." Lola left the hospital humming a tune under her breath.

⋙⋘

A week later, Lola and Sherry picked up Maria at her apartment and drove her to Gus Mendez's house. He lived in a medium-priced neighborhood. It was a neighborhood where all of the men had jobs and there were lots of children playing in the yards.

As they pulled into Gus's driveway, Maria was

impressed with the neat lawn and shrubs around the house. There was an attached garage, but Lola had a key and let them in the front door.

When they entered the house Maria saw a place where a single man lived. There were newspapers strewn everywhere in the living room, dirty dishes in the sink; however, on inspection, the bed was made in the master bedroom and the bathroom was neat and fairly clean. By Maria's standard, there was a lot of cleaning to do.

"We're going to leave you here Maria, while we go and get the lieutenant. *Profesor* Gilberto will pick up the children after their tutoring lessons and take them to the apartment. We thought the first day home, Gus would be better off without the children here. However, he said it was okay with him anytime you wanted to bring them here while you were caring for him. Sherry and I will pick up the children and take them to Lenny's ranch, and then when you are finished here we'll pick you up and take you all to your apartment. Is that all right?"

Maria smiled and hugged Sherry and Lola. "*Gracias, señoritas*, for everything you do for me."

"We love to do it, Maria," Lola said as she hugged her back.

Once the girls had left, Maria took inventory as to what she needed to accomplish before the lieutenant returned home. She began in the bedroom and changed the sheets, then put the dirty ones in the washing machine on the back porch. Maria had never been around an automatic washer and tried to figure out how it worked. Finally she had it started and closed the lid. Next, she attacked the kitchen, soaking the dishes while she scrubbed the floor. When the kitchen was in order, she picked up the papers in the living room and straightened it up, dusting the tables. On one of the tables a photograph of a lovely woman in her forties smiled back at Maria. This must have been the lieutenant's wife, Maria thought. She wiped it carefully and put it back in its place. She was sorry he had lost his wife, but a part of her was glad that she had this opportunity to be near him. She found the vacuum cleaner on the back porch, something she had never used before. There was no problem turning it on.

When everything was cleaned up and in order, she set about cooking some rice and beans and fried up a package of ground beef that Lola and Sherry had bought. She wanted food ready when the lieutenant arrived.

⋛⋚

Gus was a little anxious waiting for Lola and Sherry to pick him up at the hospital. He liked the idea of Maria being at his house and agreeing to look after him for a couple of weeks until he was back on his feet, but...he felt embarrassed at her seeing him in such a compromising position. He hadn't let a woman into his house since his wife had passed away. Deep down he knew it was time for him to find another to share his life. He still had a few good years left.

Maria was a lovely woman, very conscientious and caring with her children. He'd never known a street person before, someone who lived at the city dump. He'd seen plenty of them in the morgue. He was both anxious and excited at this new turn in his life. He had those two lovely American *señoritas* to thank for this new change. It was also because of them he had been shot and confined in the hospital. But that was part of his job; he didn't blame anyone for that.

It looked like Lily was playing cupid for him and Maria. Granted he needed someone to take care of him until he got on his feet again. And Maria was the logical person to hire. Contrary to his usual attitude of keeping people at arm's length, Lieutenant Mendez found himself personally caring about Lily, Sherry and Maria, as well as her five children. He guessed he was still in for a few surprises in life.

As the nurse finished packing his overnight case, he was ready to go home. Now where were the girls?

≥≤

*A*n hour after Lola and Sherry dropped off Maria at the lieutenant's house, they arrived at the hospital. When they entered Gus's room, he was sitting in a wheel chair looking at his watch.

"What took you so long? I thought you'd be here earlier." His words were softened by his smile.

"We had to drop Maria off at your house, and it takes an hour to drive here," Lola said. "Are you checked out?"

Gus nodded. "Yes, I've been ready since I woke up this morning."

The nurse came in and wheeled Gus to the back door. As she pushed him down the hallway he waved goodbye to the staff at the hospital.

Lola brought her VW up to the curb and the nurse helped Gus into the front seat. He leaned back on the pillow Sherry had remembered to put behind his head.

"You girls are certainly nice to come and get me. One of my associates at the station could have picked me up."

"Gus, we wouldn't let anyone else do this. We want to take you home. Maria is waiting; she probably cleaned your entire house and is fixing lunch for all of us."

"Don't know what I've done to deserve this, but I thank you both."

"Just consider it's because of your good behavior," Lola said. She and Sherry laughed and got a smile out of Gus.

On the ride back to Chihuahua Gus dozed and the girls quietly took in the scenery so as not to disturb him.

When they parked in his driveway, Gus opened his eyes. Lola got out and came around to the passenger side, and with Lola and Sherry on each side of him, he walked slowly up to his front door. Maria opened it wide and gestured toward a chair waiting for him.

"Welcome home, Lieutenant," Maria said. She patted a pillow leaning against the back and the three of them carefully helped Gus into the chair.

"Thank you, Maria; it's nice to be home." Lola took the lieutenant's bag into the bedroom and unpacked it. She laid his empty holster on the dresser, and took his dirty clothes to the laundry room.

When she returned to the living room she told Gus where she put his holster. "Where is your gun?" she asked.

"Sergeant Marin found it in on the dead man. He reclaimed it and it's down at the station."

Maria called from the kitchen; "Lunch is served."

"Can't we serve Gus in the living room, Maria?" Lola asked.

"Yes. I'll send Sherry in with a tray," Maria called.

Sherry placed a tray on Gus's lap. The aroma of the beans and beef wafted under his nose. "Boy, this smells good. I'm hungry and ready to eat something besides hospital food."

They all laughed. Lola tucked a cloth napkin under Gus's chin. "Go ahead. We'll bring our dishes in here."

Sherry appeared with two plates in her hand. She handed one to Lola. Maria sat down on the sofa and set her plate on the coffee table.

Usually Mendez did not like anyone eating in his living room, however, this seemed just fine to him. It felt like a home again.

"Gus, when you were waiting out by the tool shed, you should have told Sergeant Marin where you were. You could have been killed," Lola said, "I'm not trying to tell you your job, but you should have had Sergeant Marin with you."

Gus knew in his heart he should have called his partner for back-up. Maybe he was getting sloppy in his old age, or maybe he was in denial about his reflexes. Certainly his had slowed down a bit. He wasn't up for retirement for another five years, and the pension that policemen got in México was very small. He had some savings, but he would have to rely on the real estate investments he had made over the years to sustain him after retirement from the police force. There were several apartment buildings around the city he had bought, and he'd banked the rent he received from them. That would be enough to take care of him and a woman with five children, he mused. Oh, Lord! He was letting his imagination run wild.

"You're probably right, Lily," Gus answered. "Next time I won't hesitate to call him first."

After everyone had eaten, Maria took the plates into the kitchen and washed everything. When she was finished she came back to the living room. "Do you want to lie down for awhile?" Maria asked. Gus nodded. He was tired and he hadn't done anything but stand up a couple of times and walk from the car to the house.

Lola and Maria helped him up and into the bedroom. They laid him on the freshly made-up bed and he kicked off his house slippers. He lay back against the fluffy pillows. They smelled of lavender soap. "Thanks Maria and Lily. You seemed to have come to my rescue again."

The two women went to the living room. "Sherry and I are leaving. We will return after dinner and take you home. We'll stop by your apartment to pick up the kids. We're taking them back to the ranch."

Maria hugged the two women. "*Muchas gracias, señoritas*," she said.

Gus had a long nap and when he awoke Maria was standing beside him with a glass of iced tea. He sat up and took a sip. The tea was sweet and cool.

"*Gracias*, Maria."

"*De nada*," she said. She left the bedroom and a little while later returned. "I have heated up some dinner for you. Do you want to eat in here or come out to the table?"

"I'll come to the table if you think you can help me."

Maria took the glass from him and set it on the bedside table. Then she helped him to a standing position by putting her arms under his armpits. This brought their faces close together. Maria looked into Gus's eyes for a split second, and then looked quickly down. Gus liked what he saw in her face. She was a lovely woman.

When he was upright, she carefully put his arm around her shoulders as she placed her arm around his waist. Mendez took the first step slowly, then the second. In this way, they made it to the dining room and he sat down on a chair she had conveniently pulled out for him. Gus was savoring the earthy aroma that came from this lovely woman who was helping him walk to the table.

At first Maria's blush tinted her cheeks at the closeness to the lieutenant. But gradually she realized he was not embarrassed so why should she be?

When he was seated and pushed up to the table

she laid a bowl of vegetable and meat stew in front of him. She got his glass from the bedroom and refilled it.

"This smells wonderful, Maria. What did you put in it?"

She told him what she had combined to make the delicious stew; small pieces of lamb, potatoes, carrots, onions, and chicken broth.

"You must dish up a bowl and eat with me. I can't eat alone." Maria filled her dish and sat at the opposite end of the table.

In spite of his lack of activity Mendez was hungry. He ate with gusto and finished his bowl very quickly.

"Where did you get the money to buy the groceries, Maria?"

"*Señoritas* Lola and Sherry bought the groceries."

"Thank you, Maria." He didn't want more of a burden to fall on the girls. They had enough expense. He would give them some money next time to cover the groceries.

"*Más, Senor?*" (More) she asked.

Mendez nodded his head. Maria refilled his dish and he began eating his second helping. After he was finished, he leaned back in his chair. "That was very, very good. Thank you for your fine cooking."

Maria inclined her head in acknowledgment. "Do you want to go into the living room?" She asked.

"*Sí,*" Mendez answered. Maria approached him but did not look into his eyes. She felt suddenly shy, but tried to hide her feelings. She draped his arm across her shoulders and they hobbled into the living. She got him into his favorite chair and turned on the T. V. She left him to return to the kitchen while she finished up the evening dishes. When she joined him, she sat next to him in the other recliner. He looked over at her and smiled. This was going to work out very nicely, thought Mendez.

⋛⋚

Clint and Sherry drove into the driveway and Sherry rushed into Lenny's house. "We're getting married!" Sherry hollered.

Lola had been whipping eggs in the kitchen. Lenny was seated at the table. She looked at the happy face of her best friend and the wide smile on Clint's. "How wonderful; when?" she asked.

Sherry grabbed Lola and hugged her. "I want you to stand up with us, will you? Be my bridesmaid?" She looked at Lenny. "And Clint wants you for his best man."

"Of course," Lola answered. She looked at Lenny. She could see sadness beneath his smile. "Absolutely," he said. "When's the big occasion?"

"I want a church wedding, so we found a Protestant minister in town. You know there aren't many Protestant ministers around these parts." Sherry babbled on. She remembered Lola and Lenny's question. "In about two weeks. Just a few of Clint's friends and of course the *profesor*, Gus, Maria and the kids."

Lola poured coffee for the four of them. They took their cups into the living room. Lenny was hobbling around pretty well with his crutches.

"There is a church downtown. A very nice old man, Reverend Montes, said he would perform the ceremony," Sherry explained.

"Have you told the *profesor* or Gus yet?" Lola asked.

"No, only you two. We just decided yesterday. I haven't even told Maria."

Lenny looked at his best friend, Clint. "So you're gonna' tie the knot? Good for you." He raised his coffee cup. "Here's to the best couple I know. I wish you many years of happiness."

"I wish you the same. I love you both," Lola said, her voice cracking slightly.

When they finished their coffee Lola invited them for breakfast. "I'm making scrambled. I'll break a few more eggs and make more."

"Thanks, but we've eaten," Clint said. "Go ahead and fix breakfast." They all adjourned to the kitchen where Lola continued to whip the eggs before pouring them in the pan.

"Want to have a little get-together here after the ceremony?" Lenny asked.

He looked at Lola for confirmation. She nodded. "That would be fun. Have everyone here at Lenny's place," Lola said.

Lenny looked at Lola. "I consider this 'our' place. Especially after you decorated the living room. It has your mark on it now."

Lola smiled in spite of her slight blush. "Okay, our place. Let's have a bang-up reception here."

"Oh, thank you Lenny and Lily. That would be

terrific," Sherry said with a catch in her voice.

"What are you wearing?" Lola asked Sherry.

"I don't know yet. I thought I'd buy something new. Maybe just a summer dress; nothing fancy."

"So when do we shop?" Lola asked.

"How about tomorrow?"

"Good. I have to go to the soup kitchen this morning to help Selena. Can you come today and help me? Then we can let her off today and she and Marta can take over tomorrow?"

Sherry looked at Clint and he nodded. "I got some chores to do at the house. Then I'm picking up Chado and Federico from their tutoring lessons later."

"Want some help, Clint?" Lenny asked. "I'm getting pretty tired of sitting around here."

"Sure. You can at least ride with me and keep me company."

"Some other news too, Lily," Sherry remembered to call her. "I called my folks in Phoenix and they said Marshmallow's property, Airstream trailer, and truck sold and the lawyer sent them a check in our names for $50,000!"

"How wonderful!" Lola exclaimed. "We can plan to take a trip to Phoenix sometime soon."

"Maybe the four of us could go to Phoenix and Clint could meet my parents," Sherry suggested.

Lola looked at Lenny. "Sounds great. As soon as I can throw away this crutch, let's do it," he said.

Lola was excited at the thought of taking a trip with Lenny and Clint and Sherry. It would be a nice break for them. Lola could sign over her check to Sherry and she could cash it since Lola did not want to use the name of Lola Raines.

The girls cleaned up the breakfast dishes and then left for the soup kitchen.

≋

*T*wo weeks later, Sherry and Clint walked down the aisle. Everyone important to the two of them was there; even Selena and Marta, who helped in La Cocina de las Chicas.

Gus had an extra policeman outside the church. Sherry looked lovely in an off-the-shoulder white Mexican wedding dress that came just below her knees. She draped a silk veil over her long blond hair. Clint had given her a gorgeous three-carat diamond that morning. It sparkled on her finger like a Fourth of July fireworks. Lola thought she looked like a fairy princess.

Maria, all the children, Gus, Sergeant Marin, *Profesor* Gilberto, Lola and Lenny sat in the first two pews. Dabbing her eyes, Maria was all smiles.

When the Reverend pronounced them 'man and wife,' Clint grabbed Sherry and gave her a long kiss. Lola felt a tear roll down her cheek. She was witnessing history here, Sherry's history. Sherry had gone through a rough relationship with Greg in Mohave Valley, and then she experienced a love relationship with Ronnie only to lose him to an accident on the railroad. Lola knew it was Sherry's time for happiness.

After the ceremony, everyone drove out to Lenny's ranch and ate tacos and tamales and rice and beans that Maria had prepared for the special occasion. Clint provided Sangria for the guests.

When the last person had left—Clint and Sherry had left earlier—Maria helped Lola clean up and then Sergeant Marin drove Maria and the kids back to her apartment. He dropped Gus off last.

Lola was unusually quiet when she and Lenny retired for the night. She had been doing some serious thinking, but wasn't yet ready to share her thoughts with Lenny.

≷≷

$\mathcal{A}$ few days later, in Lenny's kitchen, Lola and Sherry were making potato salad for a picnic that afternoon. Maria and the kids, the *profesor* and Gus were invited. They would all meet at a local park in town.

"Sherry, I think we should pay Selena and her friend to work at La Cocina de las Chicas instead of just volunteering. That would free both of us up from having to be there on a regular basis. What do you think of my idea?"

Sherry nodded. "Sounds good. Clint and I want to go to Puerto Vallarta next month for a couple of weeks. Have you and Lenny considered our suggestion to go with us?"

Lola had thought about it and discussed it with Lenny. "We have talked about it and we both would like to go. The only thing is getting someone to keep an eye on our two places."

"I'll bet Gus would do it or get one of his policemen to drive by every day. Let's ask him," Sherry suggested.

"Okay," Lola said. "If he can't manage it I think he will say so. Then we'll figure something else out."

The girls put the salad in the fridge to cool. Maria was making rice and beans and enchiladas at her place.

"Let's ask him today at the picnic," Sherry said.

Lenny and Clint came in from the back yard. They had been washing cars. "When are we meeting Gus at the park?" Lenny asked.

"At two o'clock," Lola answered. "He'll pick up Maria and the kids. They'll all fit in his new van." Gus had bought a new Ford van that would conveniently hold all of Maria's family comfortably. This did not go unnoticed by Lola, Sherry, Clint or Lenny.

"Kind of interesting that Gus bought a vehicle to hold all of them, isn't it?" Sherry commented.

Lola was all smiles. "Maybe it means he has something on his mind about their future," she said.

Lenny put in his two-cent's worth. "Yeah, he asked me what I thought of him getting married again at his age. I told him I thought it was a brilliant idea." Lenny grinned.

Lola grabbed Lenny by the arm. "You didn't tell me that."

He put his arm around Lola and hugged her. "He asked me to keep it quiet until today. I think he's going to ask Maria tonight."

"Oh my God, Lily, isn't that wonderful?" Sherry crowed. She turned to Clint. "Did you know about this, too?"

Clint rolled his eyes, "Me? Why would I know anything about this?"

"Because you and Lenny tell each other everything," Lola stated.

"Maybe Lenny let something slip. I just keep my mouth shut." Clint winked at Lenny.

"How are we going to pretend we don't know at the picnic today?" Sherry exclaimed.

"You girls just calm down. Don't spoil Gus's surprise. You'll hear about it from Maria tomorrow I'm sure." Lenny advised.

The four of them sat down to smoke a joint and discuss Gus and Maria's possible wedding plans.

≷≷

*G*uido Carscione sat down to his breakfast of poached eggs, bacon, fried potatoes, cinnamon toast and dark Turkish coffee. He picked up the morning Las Vegas Herald. On the third page he saw the headline, *Las Vegas Dancer Found Dead in Mexico*. Guido continued to read.

Las Vegas exotic dancer Lola Raines-Morales was found shot to death in Chihuahua, Mexico last week. The apparent gunman was killed by the Chihuahua police department in a shoot-out. She had been on the Las Vegas police list of missing persons for over a year in connection with the death of Tony Ricco, manager of the Calendar Club Theatre and Casino. Las Vegas Police Chief Flynn said as far as he was concerned the case was closed on the death of Tony Ricco.

Lieutenant Mendez had called the Vegas Police a few days before to confirm that the Morales woman was dead. The contact in the police department called Guido right away. Guido smiled and laid down the paper. He was finally content that all the loose ends of Tony's death had been laid to rest. Too bad he had lost three hit-men in the pursuit of Lola Raines-Morales. She proved to be a hard woman to hunt down. First, Martin in Arizona shot by a do-gooder bar owner thinking she was being held up, then Jack in the shoot-out with the police in Chihuahua. The one Guido really hated to lose was Philippe. He'd learned from his Juarez contact that Philippe had been killed in an automobile accident on his way to Chihuahua. He had been a damn fine hit-man. What a waste! Guido would have to check with his New Jersey connection to see if they could ship a couple more men to Vegas. The supply of hit-men was quickly becoming depleted. Guido couldn't let that happen.

The portly but impeccably dressed crime boss of Las Vegas finished his breakfast and put in a call to New Jersey.

⧓

*L*ola and Lenny had put away the picnic leftovers, smoked a joint and headed for the bedroom. Lola climbed into bed first and watched Lenny undress. He was a wonderful-looking man, but more than that, he was a sweet, considerate and generous one. He had embraced Lola into his life without any hesitation.

All of her life she had suffered from the molestation by her father which started when she was twelve. When she went to her mother about it, years later, she had told Lola she didn't believe her. Lola had run away rather than put up with her father's advances any longer. She found she couldn't let a man get close to her after that. All of her beginning relationships fizzled after a few weeks. Her longest relationship with Lenny seemed to have a spirit of its own. She and Lenny spoke the same language. Sometimes they didn't need words to communicate and show love. But whenever he pressed her for a long term relationship, or to move in with him, she froze. When she moved to Vegas and Tony Ricco, the Vegas casino manager, came into her life, he treated her so respectfully and sweetly, she did have sex with him many times. But as far as emotional closeness, that never occurred with him. Tony didn't seem to mind. Sherry was right; she had been running away long enough.

Her memories tumbled to a stop when Lenny climbed into his side of the bed and turned out the light.

Lola cuddled up close. "Honey," she said softly.

"Hmmm?" Lenny responded.

"If you still want me for your wife, I'd really consider it an honor, because I love you very much."

Lenny was quiet for a half a millisecond. Then he turned over and grabbed her. "Do I still want you? I've always wanted you."

"I'm so glad. Could we maybe get married in Puerto Vallarta when we go with Sherry and Clint next month?"

"Halleluiah," Lenny hollered, still in a state of joy about what he'd just heard. He rocked her in his arms and planted little happy kisses on her neck, cheeks, eyelids and lips.

"Can we?" Lola repeated.

"Of course we can. I can't think of a better plan, unless you want Gus and Maria and the *profesor* at our wedding. Then we would need to have the ceremony here."

"I think just the four of us is what I want. Nothing elaborate. I need to ask Gus what name I should put on our marriage certificate."

"Listen, honey, you are no longer Lola. You are and always will be Lily from now on."

She nodded. "I know, it's just hard to get used to. I want our marriage to be authentic."

"It will be. You have proof you are Lily Elmwood already. We'll tell whoever marries us that we're cousins. That explains the same last name," Lenny suggested.

"Okay."

"We'll talk to Gus about it and he can advise us what we need to do to make sure it's recorded."

She felt better at the suggestion that they talk to Gus. He would know what to advise her. She had done some hard thinking and she knew in her heart she never wanted to be parted from Lenny. She loved him as she had never loved anyone before. The shadows that had continually reminded her of her unhappy childhood had been chased away since she'd reunited with him.

The soup kitchen was well taken care of, with Selena and Marta taking over most of the responsibilities. Now Sherry and Lily relieved *them* twice a week. Maria's children were being educated a little at a time. This was one of Lily and Sherry's better accomplishments. And Maria and Gus were getting married in three months; he was taking early retirement so he could be a father and husband.

She and Lenny would marry in Puerto Vallarta in a few weeks when the four of them traveled there on vacation. Lola Raines Morales was dead, and Lily Elmwood was born. What more could an American ex-exotic dancer, ex-frightened and abused human being desire in life? She felt suddenly complete for the first time in her life.

Lily's Elmwood's heart was full of love, contentment and happiness as she drifted into a peaceful sleep.

To order additional copies of this book: www.colleenraesnovels.com or www.createspace.com/3573743

Made in the USA
Charleston, SC
13 August 2011